Charlie's New Home

An Animal House Shelter Story

Margaret Kay

Sisters Romance

ISBN: 978-1-951199-39-5

Contents

A note about this story from Margaret Kay

This story was originally written as a short story that was included in the charity anthology, Love Latte's and Holiday Tales, which was in print for a limited time. It is no longer available. When the rights were returned to me, I knew I wanted to expand the story into what I'd originally envisioned it to be, but I'd had to cut it down to a short story of under 5,000 words for the Anthology, which isn't many words!

I am proud to present to you this expanded version of this story with much more content, more characters, and better character development with a deeper plot than the original short story. In the original, the main female character's name was Gia. I have changed it to Maeve in this book for several reasons.

First is that my sister, Charlie Roberts, published her most recent story, Seduced at Stevens Street, just 1 month before my publishing this expanded story. Her main female character was also named Gia. As I read and make suggestions on her books, edit, and format her books, the name Gia solidly belonged to the character in that story, and it no longer felt right for the character in this story.

Secondly, in expanding this story, I am able to develop the characters more deeply. From the beginning of writing the short story, I envisioned this main female character's physical traits coming from an Irish mother and a Hispanic father.

And lastly, one of my daughter's friends has a daughter named Maeve. Upon hearing the name, I fell in love with it and knew I had to use it in a story.

If you read the original short story, I hope you find this expanded version enjoyable. If this is your first time reading it, welcome to the Animal House Shelter Series. Please check out That First Year, the other book in the series at the time of this book's publication. And watch for the next planned book in the series, coming at a later date, That Second Year.

Dedication

T his book is dedicated to the real Animal House Shelter, in Huntley, Illinois.

I thank its founder, Leslie, for allowing me to use the name in this story. We adopted our beloved fur-baby from AHS. Our daughter's family has adopted from them, as has our son.

Animal House Shelter is a non-profit, no-kill 501(c)3 shelter for all breeds of dogs and cats. They rescue, care for, and find homes for homeless pets who arrive at AHS for various reasons, including:

Abuse, neglect, or abandonment
Owners whose time, income, or situation changes
Animals scheduled for euthanasia at other clinics

Once rehabilitated and ready, they are carefully matched with homes for adoption or foster care.

https://www.animalhouseshelter.com/

When looking for the next addition to your family, please visit a local shelter and consider one of the many pets looking for homes.

June

Virginia

Maeve Torres gathered her dark brown, shoulder-length hair into a ponytail. Sweat trickled down her neck. It was a warm, humid morning. Late June in Virginia usually saw average highs in the mid to upper eighties. The temperature had already reached eighty at ten a.m. The forecast was for temps to top out around ninety. There were still four cars in front of her at the drive-thru of her favorite coffee shop, and she was already late for her volunteer shift at the Animal House Shelter.

"Hounds and Grounds. What can I start for you?" the voice boomed through the speaker when she finally made it to the ordering stand.

She ordered a tall, iced vanilla latte, her summer usual. She'd pour it into her insulated tumbler and sip on it for the next hour.

Alex Richmond stepped up to the counter after waiting for fifteen minutes in the crowded coffee shop. Beside him, wearing a camouflage collar and secured on a matching camouflage leash, was his best friend, Charlie, a golden retriever. He ordered an iced coffee for himself and a frozen pup cup for Charlie. Then he took a seat on the patio in the far corner with his back to the inside of the shop. He wasn't sure how he'd get through the next hour. Every time he looked at Charlie, tears filled his blue eyes, and the incredible sadness he felt choked his breathing.

After Charlie devoured his pup cup, he licked Alex's hand, which stroked his white-blond fur. Alex called him to jump up and into his lap. He embraced him tightly. "I love you, boy," he whispered. "I am so sorry."

When he exited the Hounds and Grounds Coffee Shop patio less than an hour later, he walked Charlie on the grassy section beside the parking lot to do his business before opening the door to his old red Ford pick-up truck for them both to enter. The drive to the Animal House Shelter took only five minutes. They were there way too fast for Alex.

Sitting in the truck, not wanting to get out, more tears filled his eyes. "I love you, Charlie," he said, petting his head. "I am so sorry," he repeated. "I promise I'll be back for you. And if I don't make it back, I promise they will find you a good home."

He allowed himself to sob for a moment, and then he tamped his emotions down and forced them to stay away. He grabbed the bag with all of Charlie's things, and he willed his legs to carry him through the front doors and into the facility. His voice cracked when he asked the woman at the main desk for the shelter's owner, Elyse Laramie. She was expecting him.

"Hi, Alex," Elyse greeted, coming into the area from the back door, which he knew led to the kennels. She gave him a hug, knowing how hard this was going to be for him. They had talked at length a week earlier. Alex was about the same age as her son and, given that his own mom was so far away, she felt the need to mother him just a bit. "We're going to take good care of Charlie. Don't you worry about that."

"I know, ma'am," he forced out in a trembling voice. "Did you find a foster home for him yet? He doesn't deserve to be in a chaotic shelter for any length of time."

"I'm confident I will soon," Elyse said.

"Can I come back and get him settled and say goodbye there?" Alex asked. Tears now poured down his face.

"Sure," Elyse said. Then she led him and Charlie back to the kennel portion of the shelter. She had a solo run ready for him, complete with his name written on the info board secured to the fencing.

Maeve Torres was in one of the runs, cleaning it, while the six large dogs who were the temporary residents were in the exercise yard with potential adopters. She heard Elyse's voice and the voice of a man. He clearly sounded distraught. She took a quick peek and saw him from the back only. He was tall and had short black hair. His olive drab t-shirt clung to his well-defined shoulders and back, which heaved with each breath.

She listened to the conversation between Elyse and this man, correctly surmising he was surrendering his dog to the shelter. She tried not to judge when people did, but it was always so hard to see a dog surrendered. This one sounded different from many who just didn't have the time or money for their pets any longer. And he was genuinely upset that he was doing it.

Maeve followed a few steps behind Elyse and the man after he gave his last gut-wrenching hug to the beautiful blond golden retriever, who now sat in the kennel bearing his name. Charlie.

After one last hug from Elyse and an assurance that she'd find a good foster home for his best buddy, Alex returned to his truck where he allowed himself to cry for a few more minutes. Then he collected himself and pointed his truck towards the base in Norfolk, where he was reporting for a deployment overseas that he'd been told could last up to nine months.

"What was that surrender about?" Maeve asked Elyse. "That guy was completely devastated."

Elise explained to her that Petty Officer First Class Alex Richmond, U.S. Navy Reserves, had no one who would take Charlie. His unit was called up, and he was shipping out that afternoon. He'd tried for over a month to find a foster home for his dog. This was his last resort. He'd paid Elyse for six months' worth of fees to house and feed Charlie, with the agreement that he'd get him back when he returned. If he returned. He was an EOD Tech, Explosive Ordnance Disposal, which was a high-risk job.

"I'll foster him," Maeve volunteered. She had lost her two adopted fur babies to old age within a month of each other and really hadn't felt ready to get a new dog yet. But this would just be a foster, albeit a long-term one.

Later that afternoon, after completing the paperwork to foster Charlie, she carried his bag of toys, food, and treats to her car while leading Charlie on his leash. He walked very well on a leash. When they walked into the house, he immediately jumped up on the couch.

"Okay, I guess you got to do that at your old house," she said to Charlie.

She went over and sat beside him and stroked his soft fur. Although she'd never let her prior dogs on this couch, as it was white and expensive, she wouldn't make him get down. She'd cover it with a blanket later. Charlie had been through enough today. If he wanted to lie on her couch, he could lie on her couch. She discovered he was very well trained, though he seemed sad. Maeve was sure he was missing his master and his home. There was always an adjustment period for dogs that were newly adopted, which they told every adopter at the shelter.

A few days later, Maeve was back at Animal House. Charlie was at her house, lying on the couch when she left. This would be the first time she'd left him alone in the house. She hoped he wouldn't destroy anything. Though she really didn't think he would. He had been the perfect dog since she'd brought him home.

She pulled Charlie's file and copied down Alex Richmond's phone number and email address. She wanted to tell him she was fostering Charlie and that he was well but missed him. She'd send a few pictures of him lying on the couch or on the bed with his toys. If it were her, she'd appreciate it. Hopefully, it would bring him comfort to know that his best friend was being loved and well cared for.

She still thought about how distraught he'd been when he brought Charlie in. It tugged at her heart and brought a tear to her eyes just thinking about it. There was no doubt in her mind that he loved Charlie. And after having Charlie in her home for a few days, she understood why. He was a great dog. He was very well-behaved and very affectionate.

Hi Alex,

My name is Maeve Torres, and I am a volunteer at Animal House. I am also fostering Charlie. He is a great dog! I took him home just hours after you had to leave him, so he did not spend much time at the shelter. He has been the perfect houseguest, telling me when he has to potty and he potties outside. I work from home most days, so I am with him most every day. He seems a little sad, missing you, I'm sure. Here are a few pictures of him getting settled in. I'll try to send you pictures every so often, unless you'd prefer I didn't. If it were me, I know I'd want to be kept informed of how my fur-baby is doing. I promise I will take very good care of him until you are home, and if you don't make it back, I will keep him until he dies of old age. I've included my phone number. Please feel free to email, call, or text whenever you'd like an update on Charlie.

Maeve

It was four days before she heard back from Alex Richmond. It was a short email.

Africa

Alex had a busy few days getting settled into the barracks. The flight over had been long and uncomfortable, and he was exhausted. Operations in the field would commence the following day, which he wasn't looking forward to.

He settled into his bunk and opened his email to find the most unexpected but welcome email. A smile came to his face as he read the email from the woman who was fostering Charlie. Elyse Laramie kept her promise to find Charlie a home. She even sent pictures of

Charlie lounging on a couch and on a bed. He tapped out a quick email reply and then plugged his phone in to charge. Sleep came very easily, knowing that Charlie was being well cared for.

Hi Maeve,

Thank you for the email and pictures, and for fostering Charlie. Having to leave him at the shelter was the hardest thing I have ever had to do. If you wouldn't mind, will you stay in touch, and continue to tell me how Charlie is, and send more pictures when you have the chance?

I appreciate it.

Thanks,

Alex

Virginia

Maeve wondered where he was and how much danger he was facing. It had to be hard to be away from home and to have to surrender his best friend to a shelter like he did. She decided she'd send him a short email with a picture of Charlie daily.

She got creative with them and added little captions. One day she put an apron on him and called him to stand up at the kitchen counter with the caption *'Chef Charlie'*. Another, she had a plastic baby pool out and filled with water. He sat in it, and she put a beach ball next to him. Her caption read *'Coolin off'*.

Charlie was easy to have around. He was very well behaved, loved to snuggle, and was a good watchdog. She was having a lot of fun taking the pictures, coming up with captions, and emailing them to Alex. It quickly became part of her daily routine.

Alex would always reply and thank her. By the end of June, he'd started to reply with witty commentary on the photo that had been sent to him. She often laughed out loud as she read his emails. He had a quirky sense of humor that she enjoyed.

July

Virginia

The Fourth of July was one of Maeve's favorite holidays. She loved everything about it — the picnics, the fireworks, celebrating America's birthday. She decorated the outside of her house with flags, banners proclaiming *Freedom* and *Home of the Free, Because of the Brave.*

She woke that morning thrilled to see the forecast of sunny skies and temperatures rising into the upper eighties. Her girlfriend, Michelle, always hosted a Fourth of July party that she went to. She made her famous cheesecake in a rectangle pan, garnished with blueberries and strawberries to create an American flag design. She, of course, shared blueberries with Charlie as she decorated the cheesecake.

Then she turned her attention to Charlie. "We need to take the picture for your daddy," she said.

She had a dog shirt with an American flag on it and was happy that it fit him. She took several photos of him posing in the shirt. He was so photogenic! She logged into Canva and put the pictures in a frame with fireworks behind it. She enhanced several of the photos she'd taken by adding fun elements to them in Canva, like putting sunglasses on him and adding 'Happy 4th' text, before sending the pictures to Alex.

She took him to her girlfriend's house for the party to swim in her in-ground pool, not knowing if Charlie could swim. She was happy to find that he was a natural swimmer. She swam with him and then sat on the patio with several friends watching Charlie and Michelle's two dogs jump in the pool to go after tennis balls Michelle's husband threw. She snapped a few pictures of Charlie swimming that she'd also send to Alex. By the time the food was cooked on the grill, the three dogs were exhausted and slept in the shade of a tree in the fenced-in backyard.

"Are you going to be able to give him back to his owner when he returns?" Michelle asked as they ate. "You seem to be getting attached to him."

"I am attached to him, but I know he's someone else's dog. Honestly, I am having such a good time sending pictures of him to Alex and emailing him to tell him how Charlie is. It's become part of my daily routine already," Maeve confessed.

"What does this guy look like?" Michelle asked.

"I don't know. I saw him only from the back when he surrendered Charlie."

Michelle held her phone up. "You search for him on Facebook. I'll look on Instagram," she said with a devilish smile. Several of their girlfriends, who sat at the table with them, laughed.

"I really hadn't thought about doing that," Maeve said.

"Come on, girl," Michelle said. "Aren't you curious? I am."

The others also urged her to try to find him on social media.

Maeve had to admit that she was curious to see what he looked like, and she wanted to find out more about him. She entered his name in the search bar. Several Alex Richmonds displayed, but she knew which was the correct one right away. His profile picture was of Charlie.

"Found him," Maeve said, clicking on the picture. Michelle did not find an Instagram account.

Maeve scrolled through his pictures and his posts. He was attractive. He had a great smile on a cute face; with sparkling dark blue eyes that she noticed right away. His body was lean and well-toned, with muscles in all the right places. He was physically active and liked to hike, canoe, and go kayaking. He had pictures on his page that showed him zip-lining, paddleboarding, jet skiing, and playing a bunch of different team sports or posing in group photos with his team.

His profile said single, and there were only a handful of posts with pictures with women in them, which made sense. If he had a girl-friend, surely she would have taken Charlie when he deployed. She couldn't help but wonder why one of his friends hadn't taken Char-lie. He was such a good boy.

She also learned that when he wasn't serving in the reserves, he was a tree trimmer. There were pictures of him high in trees with a chainsaw. Maeve was in awe of him. And if she was honest, she was attracted to him. She read off what she'd found out about him and turned her phone to show Michelle and the other women pictures of him.

"He's cute," Michelle said. "And the two of you have a lot in common."

"Maybe," Maeve said. She wouldn't share that she was attracted to him.

"What are you going to do about it?" Michelle asked.

"Do about what?" Maeve returned.

"He's cute, you're writing to him almost daily, and you're taking care of his dog. That could be the basis of a relationship," Michelle said.

"Babe, stay out of it," Ron, her husband, warned when he saw Maeve's frown.

"What? Stay out of what? I'm just saying it could lead to something."

"And if it does on its own, great. If not, that's okay. It's not like I'm looking for someone," Maeve said. And she wasn't. Her last relationship had ended badly. Really badly.

"I hate to hear you say that," Michelle said. "How long are you going to be alone and let him?" she began, but Maeve interrupted her.

"Michelle, please. You know I don't want to talk about him at all."

"Aren't you lonely?" Michelle asked.

"Not in the least," Maeve said. "Now really, please, Michelle." Her voice was pleading, but it also held a warning.

"I'm sorry. I'll drop it," Michelle promised.

"Thank you," Maeve said.

The awkward moment was broken by one of their mutual friends changing the conversation to recruitment for his bowling league, which would be starting the second week of August, in just over a month. Maeve had played the year before and readily agreed, as did Michelle and her husband.

Maeve appreciated that he'd changed the subject. Everyone at the party knew about her last relationship and bad breakup with Michael. It wasn't a secret, and everyone knew she didn't want to discuss it or him. Thankfully, he'd moved out of the area, so she didn't have to run into him.

The rest of the day and early evening went fine, but Maeve would admit that she could not pull herself from the foul mood she felt because of Michelle bringing Michael up. She hated that Michelle thought she was lonely. She wasn't. Her life was very full. She didn't need a man in her life to be happy.

Not knowing how Charlie would react to the sounds of fireworks, Maeve decided to head home rather than to the city's fireworks show with the rest of her friends. She could have left Charlie at Michelle's with her dogs and picked him up after, but she wanted to be with him and be able to adjust the volume of the TV to help drown out the booms of the fireworks if he was bothered.

She sat propped up in bed with the television on loud, with Charlie curled up next to her. She opened her email and tapped out a note to Alex.

Hi again, Alex,

As I told you in my email earlier, we went to my friend's 4th of July party today. Charlie had a great day swimming at my friend's house and playing with her dogs.

They all got along great. Here are a few pictures of him jumping into the pool and swimming after the balls. We're lying in bed now, and Charlie isn't bothered at all by the firecrackers and little fireworks going off in the neighborhood. One of my previous dogs was very scared. One year, she actually wedged herself behind my washing machine; she was freaking out so badly. Anyway, I wanted to send these pictures to you. Wherever you are, I hope you got to celebrate our nation's birthday in some way.

More another day.

Maeve

Maeve stayed up for several hours watching a movie. She checked her email before turning the TV off for the night. There was an email from Alex that had just arrived.

Maeve,

Wow, I'm going to get spoiled, two emails in one day. Yes, Charlie loves to swim. That was awesome of your friend to let you bring him with you and to allow him to swim in their pool. I hope you had a good time; it looks like Charlie did. Yes, we got to celebrate some. Several guys and I pulled together an impromptu baseball game. They cooked up hamburgers and hotdogs and the cook made macaroni salad and potato salad, just like we were at a 4th of July BBQ. Thankfully, there were no fireworks, as over here, that's not a good thing. LOL. Anyway, thank you again for all the pictures of Charlie. I loved the ones you sent earlier today with him in the shirt and with the fireworks behind him. How'd you make that? Some software or graphics program, huh? Is that what you do for work? Are you a graphic artist?

Alex

Maeve read his email twice and was going to reply, but decided she'd wait until the next day to answer his question. She knew it was silly, but she didn't want to send a third email in one day. At the very least, he may think she was lonely and pathetic. Michelle's comments had really gotten to her.

When she woke up the next morning, Charlie's head was on the pillow beside her. He glanced over at her and bellied up, making her chuckle. After rubbing his tummy, she was able to get her phone and snap a couple of pictures of him before he got up. She'd send them to Alex.

While she had a cup of coffee, she re-read Alex's email from the night before. As she drafted the email to him, she had to remind herself not to mention anything she saw on his Facebook page. She didn't want him to think she'd stalked him.

Hi Alex,

Well, this is what I woke up to today, LOL. And of course I had to rub his belly. Charlie is the sweetest! To answer your question, no, I'm not a graphic designer. I just love playing around in Canva. I'm a CPA. It's kind of boring, but I'm good with numbers and it pays the bills. The firm I work for has great benefits, and I can work most days from home. I have to go into the office only three to four days a month. As I write this, I can only imagine how different it is from your job. Elyse told me you're an EOD in the Navy. I Googled that, and your job looks dangerous. Stay safe.

Maeve

Africa

Alex smiled, seeing the picture of Charlie bellied up with his head on the pillow. He always read the email first out of respect for Maeve and the fact that she not only fostered Charlie but also since she sent him pictures of his buddy and communicated with him daily. His own mother didn't do that. She text messaged or emailed maybe once a week. His mind had conjured up an image of Maeve, a fifty or sixty-something divorcee whose children were grown and gone, who thankfully opened her home and heart to Charlie.

He knew he could try to find her on social media to see if his image of her was correct, but he had no need to do that. It didn't matter who she was. All that mattered was that she took amazing care of

Charlie. And he didn't want to spoil the mental image he had of this wonderful, motherly woman who spoiled Charlie.

Alex had already decided that this would be his last deployment. He was done serving in the reserves. He was done leaving Charlie and his civilian life. When Alex transitioned to civilian life after his enlistment was up, it seemed like a good idea to stay in the reserves. He had valuable skills, and the extra money every month made life easier for him. Combined with what he'd saved when he served, this extra monthly income from the Navy Reserves enabled him to buy a small house.

But now, being back in an active unit, again seeing the carnage that explosive devices brought to human beings and animals who stumbled across them, he remembered why he'd gotten out of the military to begin with. The amount of unexploded IEDs Alex and his team found was disgusting. The thought of innocent civilians, women and children, being blown up, sickened him. That was what kept him going back out to sweep the villages each day. He didn't need to ask himself whether his job was important, or whether the mission was important. He received an answer with each device they located, removed, and detonated safely.

Parts of the world were God-forsaken hellholes. He was in one right now. It was as hot as hell, a parched landscape that didn't want to support life, that was fought over by intolerant people who wanted to destroy anyone who wasn't like them or didn't believe as they believed. They called it ethnic cleansing, which was a civilized way of saying killing anyone of a different ethnicity or religion you didn't tolerate.

His escape from the reality of his days was each night as he lay in his bunk, he brought up the email from Maeve with pictures of Charlie. It was then that he was reminded of home and of what waited for him at the end of this deployment. His best friend, Charlie, and his civilian life waited.

He had many good friends, none of whom could take Charlie for six months due to their living situation. Most lived in small apartments where big dogs weren't allowed. A few were married with children, with their own pets who didn't get along with other pets. One who really wanted to help had a daughter with severe allergies to dogs. And his parents had recently moved to Florida and lived in a condo in one of those resort-style communities with pools and a host of daily activities for the mostly senior residents. If not, they would gladly have taken Charlie as they had in the past when he had training or during the times he had reported for duty.

He wrote a reply to Maeve.

LOL, Maeve,

Yeah, I woke up to that many mornings. He'll take over the whole bed if you let him. I miss it. I miss him even though some mornings he was in my back and I was lying in a contorted position around him. If I had the computer and graphics skills you have, I'd take that pic-ture of Charlie and add text that says, yes, I rule this bed, maybe even put a crown on his head, LOL. I'd never heard of Canva and Googled it when you mentioned it. It looks like a fun program. I will be honest enough to tell you I don't have great computer skills as I don't work on one daily. I know enough to get by and do my online banking, and I'm great at Google searches, LOL. Working from home, I'd assume you are on your computer all day.

Alex

The next evening when he opened the email, he laughed out loud. Maeve had done just that. She'd taken the picture of Charlie on the bed and added a text bubble with the words, I rule this house and she put a crown on his head.

"What are you laughing at?" Darren, his teammate and friend, asked. Darren's bunk was beside his.

Alex hadn't told Darren how often Maeve wrote and sent pictures of Charlie, just that she did. He held his phone up to show Darren the picture. "The woman who is fostering Charlie created the funniest picture with him. There's a program called Canva she likes to use to make funny things with his pictures. It's entertaining."

"Sounds like she has a lot of spare time on her hands," Darren said.

Alex hoped he was joking. "Maybe, but the fact that she fills it with sending me cute things with Charlie to keep me entertained is amazing."

Virginia

July flew by. Maeve went to Michelle's to swim several days a week, taking Charlie with her each time. A teacher, Michelle, was off for the summer, and the two friends had spent many summers by her pool.

By the end of July, Maeve had a great tan. She was always grateful that she took after her father's Hispanic side of the family rather than her Irish mother's. Her mom's fair skin burned and never tanned. Like her father, Maeve tanned to a golden brown. She loved that she got red highlights in her dark brown hair when it was kissed by the sun, one great thing she'd inherited from her mother, who was a natural redhead.

"Bowling starts next week," Michelle said.

"Yes, and then you go back to school, what, two weeks later?" Maeve asked.

"Yes, don't remind me. It's been a nice break. I'm seriously reconsidering my career choice. I'd love to work from home, like you do."

Maeve laughed. "It does have its perks, like shifting the majority of my workday until later so I can come over and swim. Summer is too short." She readjusted her position on the lounge chair and gazed over at Charlie, who slept with Michelle's dogs under the tree. They had run and swum like crazy dogs for a solid hour when she and Charlie had first arrived at Michelle's.

Michelle saw her looking towards the dogs. "So, are you still emailing with Charlie's owner, the hunky tree-trimmer?" Michelle asked. She hadn't brought him up since the Fourth of July party.

"Yes," Maeve answered, bracing herself for Michelle's comments that were sure to follow.

"Look, I'm sorry I said what I said on the fourth. I could blame it on the margaritas, but the truth is I'd so like to see you with a nice guy. You deserve your happily ever after, Maeve."

"My happily ever after, huh? I think you've read too many romance novels this summer." She laughed. "I'm seriously not looking."

"They're not all snakes, like Michael," Michelle said.

Maeve felt her body go rigid at the mention of his name. That was proof to her that she wasn't ready for another relationship yet. "Just hearing his name gives me a visceral reaction."

"I'm sorry," Michelle apologized. "Is it wrong that I want my best friend to be happy?"

Maeve turned her head to the side so that she gazed at Michelle. "Thank you for wanting that. And I am happy. I don't need a man in my life. I believe that we make our own happiness."

"Absolutely, but having a good man in your life who loves and supports you elevates you to a different level of happiness, that's all. And I want that for you."

"You did luck out with Ron. He's a great guy." Then Maeve chuckled. "But just admit it. You want another couple to travel with and to go out with on a regular basis."

Now Michelle laughed. "Well, yeah, that too."

"I'm just glad that the three of us still go out."

"Me too. Ron's cool that way, doesn't mind being out with two women," Michelle said, laughing.

What Maeve did not tell Michelle was that she had what she would describe as a one-sided romance with Alex. She looked forward to his emails each day. She spent a lot of time planning her emails to him and the pictures of Charlie she'd send. Was it possible to really be falling for someone you'd never met? Silly, she knew. Besides what she viewed on his social media pages; she knew little about him. And she spent a lot of time looking through his Facebook posts, visiting his page often. He had no new posts since he'd deployed. She assumed he wasn't allowed to post anything about it.

August

Africa

Alex continued to look forward to the daily emails from Maeve. The pictures of Charlie with the cute captions always made him smile. Opening the email was the best part of his day, so he usually saved it until he was in his rack and about to go to sleep. He liked that she spoiled Charlie. He deserved that. From the little bits that he saw of the home Charlie was living in, it looked nice. There was a fenced-in backyard for Charlie to play in and remain safe. Everything looked clean and well-kept, and it was decorated nicely.

Then came the day that he caught a glimpse of the woman behind the phone, taking the pictures of Charlie. Her reflection, captured in the sliding glass door behind Charlie, displayed her. She was gorgeous and looked to be in her early to mid-thirties, the same as him. She had dark hair that was piled on top of her head in a messy bun. Her facial bone structure was perfectly feminine, with what looked to be a flawless, darkly tanned complexion. She had big brown eyes that sparkled as her full lips displayed a beautiful smile. Her body looked toned but had ample curves that drew his gaze.

He stared at her picture, memorizing everything about her. Yes, he'd admit he was immediately attracted to her. And to think Charlie had been lying beside her in bed, snuggled up with her for the past few months. Lucky dog.

"Well hello, Maeve Torres," he said aloud. Why had he assumed she was fifty or sixty-something?

He opened his Facebook app and searched for her, unsure why he hadn't before now. When he found her, he spent an hour looking over every post, every picture on her page. He didn't see a significant other. But what he did see was a beautiful woman who was physically active, liked a lot of the same activities he did, and had what looked to be a group of good friends she did things with on a regular basis.

He didn't mention seeing her in the picture in his reply to the email, even though he really wanted to say something about it being nice to see her in the picture. And of course he didn't admit to stalking her on social media. But he wrote more to her that night than he had yet.

Maeve,

That picture of Charlie in the bathtub made me laugh. I remember his first bath, when I brought him home from Animal House. He was so tiny he fit in my kitchen sink. He smelled something terrible when I adopted him, so I had to bathe him right away, and he loved the water even then. He was so cute as a puppy. You have provided me with your phone number in every email, so if you don't mind, I'll text you his puppy pictures. I hate to admit

I'm not very tech-savvy. I'm not sure how to attach a pic to an email, but I can text one. I work as a tree trimmer. The company I work for has a contract with the local utility companies. Yeah, I'm one of those guys who goes up in lifts or climbs the trees to keep them trimmed so their branches don't bring down power lines. So, what I'm saying is, I don't spend all day on my computer like you do as a CPA. Back to Charlie, he was the cutest of his litter. When I went to look for a puppy to adopt, I sat in the middle of the room, and he came over and picked me, sat on my lap and didn't get up. And just like he does with you in bed, he snuggled with me from that first night. As a puppy, he trained so easily and quickly. He really is the best dog.

Alex

Virginia

Maeve laughed out loud when she read Alex's reply to the email with the picture that she'd accidentally captured her reflection in. She'd been very careful not to have her image in any of the pictures of Charlie she'd sent until that point. She hadn't included it on purpose, but when she saw her reflection on the door, she didn't delete it and retake it either. Though he didn't mention that she was in the photo, he wrote a longer email than usual. He seemed more open, talking about more personal stuff.

Without thinking, she drafted a purely personal email.

Alex,

I adopted both of my last dogs from Animal House too.
They had been surrendered at about six years old by their
owner because she had to move and couldn't take them
with her. She'd lost her job and then her house and was
moving in with her sister in Boston, into an apartment
that didn't allow dogs. They were a bonded pair and had
to stay together. I was a volunteer at Animal House, and
I instantly fell in love with them both. I have volunteered
at Animal House for about four years. I get so much
satisfaction from working there. And after I lost both
of them to old age, I didn't feel ready for another dog
yet, but going in and playing with the dogs or working
to clean their kennels makes me feel good. And since I
work from home most of the time and I live alone, the
time I spend at Animal House gives me contact with
people. LOL, that sounded like I'm a recluse. I'm not.
I have many good friends. I play in a bowling league
on Thursday nights in the fall through early spring. I
play sand volleyball with friends at a sports bar during
the summer, and I am part of a running club, currently
training for my next 5K. I'll be honest, I overheard you
when you brought Charlie in, and it broke my heart that
you had to leave him. That's why I told Elyse I'd foster
him, and I'm so glad I did.

Maeve

After she hit send, she second-guessed sending him an email about herself rather than Charlie. She wasn't sure where to go in the next email. Would she make it more personal or go back to it being just sharing pictures of Charlie? She guessed she'd need to see how he responded to decide.

Africa

Alex read Maeve's email twice before going to sleep. It was wonderful to read more about her. She shared her life, her thoughts, and losing her last dogs with him. He wanted to reply, but he stopped himself. He had to think about what deepening their conversation would mean.

He knew himself. He wanted a long-term relationship with a woman that would lead to marriage and children, and he knew what it would mean to him if he got to know her and liked her more than he already did. Was it smart to go down that road right now?

When he replied to her the next day, his email was just as personal. He'd made his decision that day as he was on patrol. He'd open himself up to her and get to know her better. If not now, when? In some ways, it was safer to do it now, through email. There was no pressure for him to ask her out. They could just remain friends.

Hi Maeve,

It was nice to read about you in that email. And honestly, it was nice seeing you in that last picture you sent of Charlie. I had wondered about you, the mysterious Maeve, dog lover, and my hero for taking Charlie in and sending me so many great pictures of him. I say dog lover as you must be to volunteer at the shelter and because you obviously understood how much I miss him to send me pictures of him almost every day. That has helped me so much, thank you! I never thought about how working from home could make a person want to do things specifically to get out and to see and talk to people. But it sounds like you get out and do a lot of things. Okay, confession time, I looked you up on Facebook. I have to ask about the sand volleyball. Are the pictures on your page from The Sports Spot? It sure looked like it. I played there as a sub on a friend's team on five occasions for his Thursday league last summer. If you played last year, I probably played against your team at least once! And I also saw you ran the Shamrock Shuffle 5K in Norfolk this past March. I did too! Small world! Look up my Facebook page. I'll be easy to find. I'm the Alex Richmond with Charlie as my profile picture. I mention the Reserves, but obviously I have nothing posted that I'm on deployment. We're not allowed to do that for operational security. But you'll see me in trees at work, and a few Reserve pictures with my unit. (That's if you're wondering what I look like.) And I have lots of pictures of Charlie on my page.

Alex

Virginia

"Holy shit," Maeve said aloud to Charlie as she read the email from Alex. Charlie lay at her feet. She was at her desk working.

Alex really put the ball in her court, didn't he? It was as though he knew what her motives were in drafting that last email and making it more about herself. She had to read it a few times to take it all in. She was shocked to read that he had played sand volleyball at The Sports Spot last summer. Yes, she had played every Thursday evening from the first week of June through the end of August, just like this year, so she had to have played against Alex at some point. She didn't remember him, but she hadn't been looking at men last year, as she was engaged to Michael and, unlike him, she was faithful to the person she dated and planned to marry.

"Don't go there with your thoughts, Maeve," she said aloud to herself.

She'd worked very hard to get herself out of that dark place she'd been in after she broke off the engagement, a place of anger and hurt. It was not a productive place to exist, and she would not allow herself to slip back into it. Most of the time, she was successful, and she tried to remind herself that it was better to find out he was a cheat before she married him. It would have been far worse to learn what kind of man he really was after the wedding or even worse if they'd had kids.

"Well, Charlie, your master did what I really didn't expect him to do. But why wouldn't it be a good idea to get to know him better? At the very least, after he comes back, it would be nice to at least be friends so that I can still see you." She leaned down and gave him a hug. She knew she would miss him terribly when Alex returned home and claimed him.

Maeve hit reply and drafted her email and also opened her Facebook app to take another look at his page. She had a picture she'd taken that morning of Charlie lying on the lounge chair in the backyard. She'd added the caption *Just Sunning'* earlier to ready it to send to Alex.

Hi Alex,

Wow, it is a small world! Yes, The Sports Spot is exactly where I play sand volleyball, and yes, I played all summer last year on Thursday nights. Which team did you sub for, and who is your friend? Maybe I know him or her. It would be wild if we had mutual friends or acquaintances. What was your time in running the Shamrock Shuffle this year? I finished it in 38:53. LOL, I just want to see how far apart our times were and determine if we possibly were in the same area at the same time after the run. I checked out your Facebook page and, of course, loved all the pictures of Charlie. Those pics of you up in the trees are crazy! I don't have a fear of heights (have also rock climbed and ziplined, love both!) but I have to say dangling up there with a chainsaw looks a little scary. I see you paddle board. I haven't ever tried it, though I'd like to learn. Where were you at while doing it? It looks tropical with the beautiful aqua-colored water. That's not at Virginia Beach with water that pretty, LOL. I haven't had a vacation away anywhere fun in a few years. My parents moved to Arizona to retire five years ago, and that's where I've gone to visit them on all but one vacation since they moved. I was born and raised in Suffolk and graduated from Lakeland High School. I went to college at Norfolk State, so I've always lived in the area.

What about you? Did the Navy bring you here, or are you a local?

Maeve

Before she hit send on the email, she called Charlie to jump into her lap, and she took a selfie of her and Charlie. She'd turned in her chair enough that her desk was in the shot. She added it to the email and hit send. She would send the picture of Charlie on the lounge chair tomorrow.

Africa

Alex enjoyed Maeve's email and learning so much about her. She didn't put what year she graduated, but he assumed it had to be relatively close to the year he did. He'd gone to high school in Suffolk too, but at a different high school. His dad was in the Navy when Alex was younger. He separated and got a job at the base as a civilian by the time Alex was in third grade, which had been awesome for Alex and his sister to actually stay in one place for more than a few years.

Wow, that was what came to Alex's mind when he saw the picture of Maeve and Charlie. Her smile was beautiful. She was beautiful. He felt like he was being given this rare look into her personal life, seeing her desk and computer and the couch across from her desk, which he knew from past emails was where Charlie lay most of the time while she worked.

Hi Maeve,

So odd I don't recognize you. I've had to have seen you around. I finished the Shamrock Shuffle in 23:39, just fifteen minutes ahead of you. I probably wasn't hanging around the finish line still when you crossed it though, but I could have been in the parking lot for at least twenty minutes after you finished. The friend whose team I've subbed on for sand volleyball is a guy I used to work with at a past job, Steve Mills. I think the team name is the Sand Crabs. Sound familiar? I graduated from King's Fork High School in 2007. I played football and basketball, and I know our teams played against yours. What year did you graduate? I know Steve graduated from Lakeland in 2006.

Alex

He hit send and hoped he'd get a reply before he fell asleep. He didn't.

Virginia

Maeve's afternoon was crazy-busy with an unscheduled video meeting with her boss, Chad Mills, and the other CPAs who worked remotely. In what was unexpected and unprecedented, Chad assigned them each to conduct a peer audit of another team member's work. She wasn't buying her boss saying it was just a quality review. Something was up. As far as she was concerned, any audits should be performed by Chad. None of her co-workers should be reviewing her work just as she shouldn't review theirs.

She spent just over two hours on the audit she'd been assigned, a file of one of the firm's long-term customers, a client assigned to her co-worker Dave Ewing. She found a few items she would have handled differently, but nothing done outright incorrectly. Many entries in accounting were a judgement call as to which category they were recorded under.

Finally at six p.m., she sent her audit summary to Chad. She popped a plate of leftovers in the microwave and poured herself a glass of wine, wanting to unwind and relax. Then she opened her email and checked for a return message from Alex.

"Are you kidding me?" Maeve said, reading Alex's email.

Steve Mills was not only her boss Chad's younger brother, but he was also an old high school friend of her brother's. It was through her brother and Steve that she had heard about her current job. Back then, Chad was just another account manager. He'd been promoted to supervisor two years earlier. Steve and her brother graduated the same year. They'd played on the same sports teams all their lives, from recreational leagues as youngsters through varsity in high school. Alex was a year younger than her brother and Steve, which would make him 36 years old, just two years older than she was.

Alex,

You are not going to believe this, but yes, I know Steve Mills very well, and I know his team, the Sandy Crabs. We play them often, which you'd expect as there are only six teams that rotate playing each other on Thursdays. Steve was also a good friend of my brother's growing up and all through high school. Although my brother moved to Chicago several years ago, they're still in touch. I guess that theory of one or two degrees of separation is true. Of course, Suffolk really isn't that large of a city; I'd be more surprised if we didn't know any of the same people. So now I'm racking my brain to access memories from volleyball last summer to try to remember you. LOL, were you any good at volleyball? And you aren't an ass when you play and spike the ball in women's faces, are you? There's been a couple of guys out for blood that we've played against. Not cool. You asked what year I graduated high school, 2009. I played a few sports, did a couple of plays, and sang in the choir, nothing note-worthy. I did enough extracurricular activities to keep my parents happy. For some reason, that was important to them. My brother, Ricky, was the jock in the family. We went to almost every game. Every Friday night in the fall we were at his football games. We went to many at King's Fork.

More later,

Maeve

She ended it there and attached the picture of Charlie on the lounge chair she'd taken and readied the day before. Then she hit send. Dying to know more about what kind of man Alex was, she opened her contact list on her phone and dialed Steve Mills.

"Hey there, stranger," Steve answered.

"Hi Steve. It's been a minute, hasn't it?"

"Everything's okay with Ricky, isn't it?"

"Yes, he's fine," Maeve said. "I talked with him last weekend. You know Ricky, working hard, gotta climb that ladder and be head of the department."

Steve laughed. "Okay, good, and yeah, he's determined to make department head before he's forty. I was sad to hear that he and Vicky broke up. I liked her, and I thought she was good for him."

"Yeah, I thought the same, but you never know what's going on inside someone's relationship," Maeve said. But she had really liked Vicky and hoped she would become her sister-in-law. "How are Stevie and Scotty doing?" she asked. Stevie was short for Stephanie, his daughter, and Scotty was his son from his marriage, which ended two years earlier in divorce. Maeve was sad for all four of them, but it sounded like Steve and his ex had a good relationship and he was a constant in his kids' lives.

"They're good, thanks for asking. Jill is bringing them to The Sports Spot this week for the game."

"That's great to hear. It'll be good to see them," Maeve said.

"I might as well tell you; you'll notice, Jill and I are kind of back together," Steve said.

"You are?" she asked, quite surprised. "That's great, Steve."

"Yeah, it's been good. We've both grown up and realized our problems weren't insurmountable, and our being together is really better for the kids. We haven't moved back in together yet, but we will soon," Steve said.

"I'm really happy for you all, Steve."

"So, why the call? Not that I mind," he said.

Now that she was about to ask him, she was feeling a bit foolish about calling. Did she really want to open herself up to questions regarding her motives?

"Maeve, you there?"

"Yes, sorry. Hey, I wanted to ask you about someone you used to work with. Do you know Alex Richmond?"

"Alex, yeah! He's a nice guy. Are you seeing him?" He sounded happy at the prospect.

"No, no, nothing like that."

"Then how do you know him and why are you asking me about him?"

Maeve thought about it for a second. She didn't want to violate Alex's privacy by telling Steve it all because it was a negative. Who surrenders their dog at a shelter?

"Maeve?" Steve prompted her again when she'd gone silent.

"You know I volunteer at Animal House Shelter, right?"

"Yeah," Steve said after she paused.

"I don't want you to think badly of him because of what I'm going to tell you; he had no choice. So, he deployed with his unit someplace overseas for like six months and he had no one to take his dog, so Alex brought Charlie to Animal House so he could be placed in a foster home until Alex gets back and I'm fostering Charlie."

"Holy shit, really? I didn't know he'd deployed. Oh, man, that had to kill Alex having to do that. He loves that dog."

"Yeah, he does, and it did devastate him."

"He's not a bad guy; don't assume he is because he gave his dog over to the shelter."

"I'm not. He loves Charlie, and he gets Charlie back when he returns. It's a temporary foster. But I'm asking because I've been sending pictures of Charlie to his email and conversing with him, and we just discovered we both knew you, and I wanted to ask about him, that's all."

"Ah, you wanted to ask about him," Steve said with meaning.

"No, I mean, maybe," Maeve admitted. "He seems nice, and I've really enjoyed emailing with him, but I wanted to find out more about him, from you, before I take it any farther and get to know him better."

"I can see you two together," Steve said. "You two have a lot in common."

"Yes, so I'm discovering. I don't remember him playing on your volleyball team as a sub, but last summer I was pretty distracted with Michael and planning our wedding until, well, you know what happened."

"Michael was an idiot; no, let me make that stronger. He was a worthless piece of cheating shit that you are too good for. When I found out what he did to you, I wanted to pound his head in, a surrogate for Ricky doing it."

Maeve chuckled. "Well, between you and me, you have a better chance of doing that to someone than my brother, but seriously, karma will get him."

"Amen, sister," Steve said. "Speaking of pieces of shit, did Alex tell you about his last girlfriend?"

"No," Maeve said. "We don't really know each other that well."

"I shouldn't say anything, but let me just say this. She hated dogs, and Alex had to make a choice between her and Charlie."

"Really?" Maeve asked. "Well, since Charlie is still in the picture and she's not, I can figure out what choice he made."

"Do me a favor and don't tell him I said anything," Steve said.

"Deal." Maeve laughed. "I was going to ask you to do me a favor too and not tell him I asked about him."

Steve laughed. "We'll both keep our mouths closed. But seriously, Maeve, he's a good guy, and I can see you two together. Give him a chance."

"Thanks, Steve, I appreciate you telling me about him."

They talked for a few more minutes about volleyball and then said goodbye. When Maeve disconnected the call, she felt much better about her decision not only to ask Steve about Alex but also about opening herself up to Alex. She was heading down the path of getting to know him better, which she knew would lead to deeper feelings for him. And with deeper feelings, there was the potential for a harder fall if he didn't feel the same or if he turned out to be someone she didn't think he was. It was one thing to have a one-sided crush on him that he didn't know about. It was another to share so much about herself that he could reject her, which would hurt.

Africa

Patrol had been long and emotionally draining. But Alex looked forward to opening his email to see if Maeve had replied. He got the normal little adrenaline rush when he saw the new email from her waiting. He lay flat on his back in his rack and read every word twice. So, she knew Steve Mills. Finally, someone in common that they both knew. As she'd said, there had to be someone. Torres, he thought hard to remember a guy from the Lakeland Cavaliers teams that had played alongside Steve Mills with that name. Of course he didn't know Steve Mills then, it was later, after his discharge from the Navy that he met him, but the two of them definitely remembered each other from their opposing high school team days, not that the two schools had a brutal rivalry. He had a vague recollection of a wide receiver on the varsity football team by that name. He wondered if he was Maeve's brother.

He had to smile when he read her commentary about guys who spike the volleyball at women's faces. He couldn't agree more. It was not cool at all, but he'd use more colorful language to describe a guy who did that. He really wished he'd been introduced to her back then. He was sure they would have hit it off.

He drafted a return email, a short one because he was exhausted. Then he passed out.

Virginia

The next day, Maeve sat at her desk working. She'd set her phone, so that incoming emails to her personal account would sound a chime to alert her one had arrived. She wanted to read Alex's return email as soon as it came in. She had a vague idea of where he was based on the time change and the fact that he said he read her emails and wrote her before going to sleep each day, which was in the afternoon her time.

Finally, the alert sounded, and she picked her phone up to read his email.

Hi Maeve,

Today was an exhausting day. It was very nice to have your email and the picture of Charlie to look at before bed. I should have known that Steve Mills would be the one person we both knew, LOL. And to answer your question about volleyball, no, I would never spike a ball at anyone's face. Definitely not a cool thing for anyone to do in recreational volleyball! I'm sorry to cut this short, but I am beat.

More tomorrow,

Alex

Maeve would admit she was disappointed by the short email. She'd hoped for more, but he did say he was exhausted. She put her phone back on the desk and got back to work. She'd email him later. She had a meeting with Chad she was preparing for.

September

Virginia

Maeve floated on her back with her head on a noodle, her gaze on the beautiful azure-colored sky. The water was warm, the sun hot, and she felt at peace. She only felt safe on her back because the dogs were out of the pool, worn out from running, swimming, and fetching tennis balls for well over an hour nonstop. They'd be up for round two before too long, she was sure.

"I'm bummed you'll be closing down the pool soon," Maeve said to Michelle, who lounged on a raft beside her.

"I'm bummed that the nighttime temps will cool off the water so that it will soon be too cool to swim," Michelle said. "But it's so expensive to run the heater. And really by mid-September, I'm over taking care of it and having wet dogs come in. I can't keep them out of it."

Maeve laughed. "They do love to swim."

"We're not closing it for two weeks yet. Plan on coming back next weekend to swim."

"I'll do that. I will say, though, that I'm looking forward to bonfires and getting my flannel out."

"Are you going to The Sports Spot's Labor Day party tomorrow?" Michelle asked. "They're having a bonfire this year and a band."

"Yes, Steve and Jill Mills will be there, and I told Steve I'd come."

"I can't believe they got back together," Michelle said. "I think it's great they reconciled, but to get back together after divorcing is very rare."

"I Googled it. It's like six percent of people who divorce get back together and remarry. If they can make it, great for them," Maeve said. "Did I tell you that Steve knows Alex?"

"No, you didn't. How'd that come up?"

"Well, Alex and I have been emailing a lot about ourselves, not just Charlie. He looked at my Facebook page and saw my pictures from volleyball and recognized The Sports Spot. He told me he played on a friend's team a few times as a sub last year, and it turns out it was Steve's team he played on."

"Small world," Michelle said. "So, did you ask Steve about him?"

Maeve turned her head and stared at Michelle without answering. The expression on her face told Michelle the answer.

"You did!" Michelle laughed.

Maeve laughed with her. "Okay, yes, I did. I was curious to find out what kind of guy he is."

There was a pause. "And come on, girl, don't leave me hanging."

Maeve laughed again. "I could be mean and not tell you." She laughed harder.

"That would be mean. Come on. Spill it!"

"Okay, okay. Steve said he's a really nice guy. He said he could see the two of us together. We like many of the same things. Alex even ran the Shamrock Shuffle this past March, finished fifteen minutes before I did. It's weird; we've like been near each other so many times over the years, like with volleyball and the 5K. He played football and basketball in high school at the same time Ricky and Steve did, but he went to King's Fork. I have vivid memories of being at those games, cheering the Cavaliers on when they played the Bulldogs."

"But you don't remember him?"

"No. I wish I had noticed him," Maeve admitted.

"Sounds like someone's crushing on him."

"Not necessarily crushing," Maeve said. "But I will admit I like emailing with him and finding out more about him. He's got a quirky sense of humor that comes through even in emails."

"And he's got a cute face too," Michelle said. "His body isn't bad either."

"Stop," Maeve said, turning red in the face. But yes, he did have a cute face and a nice body. She wouldn't argue about it.

Maeve didn't check her email until after she and Charlie got home. They'd stayed at Michelle's for dinner. She put on her pajamas and turned on the television in her room and then sat against her backrest pillow. Charlie curled up beside her.

She opened her email and got the same warm feeling she always experienced when she saw his name in the email list. She clicked on his name and read his email.

Maeve,

Happy Labor Day to you too. I worked most of the day, but the cooks did make picnic-style food for us when we got back from patrol. They try to keep morale up through food, LOL, or in matching the food to the holiday back home. You asked for my mailing address over here. I've included the FPO address to reach me at the bottom of this email. You also asked me in that last email why I joined the Navy. I'd say pretty much the same reason most other people do. I wanted to serve my country, which I'm sure sounds hokey or predictable. My father and both of my grandfathers served, and I was raised to believe it was the right thing to do. Also, when I graduated from high school, I didn't have a career in mind. I didn't want to go to college without a major, and if I'm being honest, I really didn't want to go to college at all. And your unasked question, why EOD tech, well, first I qualified for it, which not everyone does. I really liked the challenging nature of the program and the fact that the job requires so many skills. Underwater ordnance is a key component. I've always loved anything water related like snorkeling, scuba, you name it. I was already PADI dive certified in high school. LOL looking back, my Navy schools to train for it were more intense than any college class could be. The training for the program was forty-four weeks long. Bet you didn't know EOD techs go through many of the same schools Navy

SEALs do. We directly support the SEALs and other special forces units. I had always wanted to parachute, and when I found out that was one of the schools and was a part of the job, that sealed the deal for me. You didn't ask, but your next question I anticipate would be, why did I get out of active duty, and why did I stay in the reserves? Being on this deployment has reminded me why I didn't re-up when my second enlistment was up. Yes, I was active duty for twelve years. I did two six-year enlistments, from the time I was eighteen until I was thirty years old. I've always loved the job. I love the camaraderie of the unit. What I don't love is how devastating exploding ordnance is to civilians or animals who happen upon it or more often to armed forces personnel who trip it. Preventing them from exploding and saving lives is why I do it but seeing the carnage when we're too late is horrible. That was why I stopped doing it as a full-time job. I have so many years in, staying in the reserves and getting a pension seemed the logical thing to do. I could still do the reserves and not do it in this capacity. EOD is voluntary, and I could walk away from it at any time. I don't know. I'll have to evaluate that after this deployment. Okay, sorry, that all went a bit darker than I anticipated. Let me turn that question around on you. Why accounting? And what do you love and hate about your job?

Alex

A somber feeling settled over Maeve. Wow, he had been very open and honest. She would admit that she didn't know much about what an EOD did beyond what she'd learned previously when she'd Googled it. She found a few YouTube videos about the training and the job she watched. After watching them, she completely respected the men and women who did that job. And she now respected Alex on a different level than she had, knowing what training he had and what job he had done for twelve years, the same job he was deployed doing now. It was dangerous, very dangerous. In one of the videos she watched they showed a wall of pictures, EOD Techs who'd died doing the job. There were a lot of pictures.

She didn't even know what to say in reply to his email. And telling him about her job seemed stupid compared to what he'd just shared about his. She'd asked for an address for him as she planned to make him some cookies and mail them to him. In one of his emails, he'd mentioned his favorite cookie was chocolate chip peanut butter cookies and how he couldn't get them where he was. She was going to make a batch for him. Even that seemed like a silly idea now.

Charlie jumped into her lap and licked her face. She held him and petted his soft coat. "What do you think? Should I still make him the cookies?" she asked Charlie.

He licked her again.

She had a friend who was married to a man in the Navy. Only one, which now seemed odd to her, living so close to the base in Norfolk. Her friend Jeannie lived in Florida now. Her husband had accepted orders to NAS Jacksonville. Maeve also knew her husband had been deployed before.

Maeve picked up her phone and tapped out a quick text to her. She could ask Jeannie what she thought about the cookies idea without fear of ridicule or endless questions about the guy she was sending them to. Jeannie was chill like that.

Maeve was a little surprised to receive a call from Jeannie rather than a return text. "Hello."

"Hi, surprise. How are you?" Jeannie asked.

In the background, Maeve could hear the ruckus of Jeannie's twin boys, who had to be three by now. "Hi lady, you didn't have to call. I know you're always busy. Do I hear the boys in the background?"

"You mean Wildman and Destructor?" Jeannie asked with a laugh. "Yes, sorry. They're just playing, and they're never quiet. But they're contained, so I have a few minutes to chat. To answer your question, yes, anything from home you can send to a guy deployed will be so appreciated. His favorite cookies? He'll love you forever!"

Maeve laughed. "He's just a friend, and I just don't want him to think it's lame or silly that I'm sending them, but he mentioned missing a specific type of cookie, and I thought he might like to have some."

"Just a friend, huh?" Jeannie asked. "Well, it's very nice of you to think about doing it for your friend. I do that kind of thing for Jay whenever he's gone. Now, I also put cheesy artwork from the kids in there, and I've sent magazines I know he likes and candy. The guys love to get candy too."

Maeve chuckled again. "Okay, thanks, that helps me make my decision. So, is Jay home or away right now?"

"He's home this week, which is good because I'm ovulating. We're trying to get pregnant again. The boys want a baby sister."

"The boys do, huh?"

Jeannie laughed. "Okay, I want a baby girl."

"You may end up with another boy, you know."

"Yeah, some women are just destined to be boy moms."

Maeve heard a loud crash and then even louder crying.

"Oh crap, sorry, got to go. I'll talk to you later." Jeannie disconnected the call.

Maeve texted a quick message to her.

> Hope all is okay, and no one is hurt too badly. It was nice chatting and thanks for the info.

Then her gaze fell again on Charlie. "Okay, she said yes to the cookies. We're going to make cookies tonight, boy."

She opened her email back up and copied down the address to get the package to Alex. Then, she replied to his email before getting out the ingredients to make the cookies.

Africa

Alex was disappointed there wasn't an email from Maeve after dinner when he reclined on his bunk. She must have had a busy day, he told himself. She had told him she'd planned to take Charlie swimming again at her friend Michelle's house. He wondered if she'd read his email he'd sent the night before. He'd second-guessed sending it after he'd tapped it out as they'd kept their conversations light, and that email was not. But he decided to go ahead and send it. He hoped that hadn't been a turnoff for her, hearing so much about the downside of his job.

He checked his email at lunch. His heart did a little flip in his chest, seeing her name in the inbox. He opened it and read it.

Alex,

Thank you for your last email and everything you shared with me. I have to say I honestly didn't know all you did or the training you had outside of the obvious of what comes to mind when someone says explosive ordnance disposal. I Googled it and read all about it and watched a couple of YouTube videos too. I knew it was a dangerous job, but I didn't know how dangerous. Some of the stuff I saw was amazing. You really jump out of planes and helicopters? And use robots to detect IEDs? I figured the scuba diving part was included but had no idea about the rest. Again, I'm really happy you shared this with me.

My job seems insignificant compared to yours, but I'll answer anyway. You asked why accounting. It's something I've always been good at. It just made sense to my brain when I learned it in high school. And it's pretty much a recession-proof job. People always need accountants, be it for businesses or individuals to prepare their taxes, though online TurboTax is doing the job for people with easy filings now. I work with business clients who aren't big enough to need in-house staff. It's not exciting work, but it's steady with a decent paycheck, and the firm I work for has good benefits. What do I like most about it? Besides working from home, I like that I have formed relationships with my clients. They know me and know I'm doing a good job for them. They trust me with their finances. I'd have to say what I like least is that it can be boring. It's the same thing all the time. When it's tax time, it's busy, and there are hard deadlines, so sometimes the overtime is brutal. But there isn't any job I'd rather be doing that I know of right now. If I won the lottery, I'd quit my job and invest in Animal House Shelter to make it bigger to help more dogs and cats, and I'd work there more days a week. And I'd travel. There's a lot of places I've never been that I'd like to see.

It's getting late, and I need to go. Charlie and I stayed for dinner at Michelle's house. We had fun swimming, one of the last days of the season. I'll email you tomorrow.

Maeve

Alex re-read it a second time and smiled, seeing the pictures of Charlie swimming with Michelle's dogs and then all three of them lying under the tree. Charlie had friends.

Darren took the seat beside him. "Whatcha reading? And why do you have a goofy smile on your face? It's from that woman who's watching Charlie, isn't it? Alex has a girlfriend," he teased.

"I've never met her, and she's just a friend," Alex insisted. Alex had admitted to Darren that he'd stalked her on Facebook, and he'd shown him her picture.

"You don't know; you may be getting catfished. She may not be the woman in the pictures." He laughed.

"She's definitely the woman in the pictures. We actually have a mutual friend."

"And did you ask him about her?"

"Not yet," Alex said. "I figured I would before we go home. But from Facebook and the pictures she's sending of herself with Charlie, I know she's who she says she is."

"So now she's sending pictures of herself with Charlie?" Darren asked, a grin on his face.

Alex laughed. "Yes, there's been a few."

What he didn't tell Darren was that she was killing him with the pictures. There was one she'd sent of Charlie lying across her legs in bed. Her toenails were painted with red polish, which immediately drew his gaze. Her legs were tanned and looked great, and all he could think of was lucky Charlie! He'd kill to be lying in bed with her. There was another picture, a selfie with Charlie's face beside hers, and the shirt she wore was kind of low cut, displaying really nice cleavage. And of course, her beautiful smile got him too. He was very attracted to her.

They had an afternoon patrol, but that night when Alex again lay in his bunk, he read her email a third time before hitting reply.

Maeve,

Charlie looks like he had a great time with Michelle's dogs. Looks like the three of them are buddies. I'm so proud; my boy has friends. I hope they're not bad influences on him, ha-ha. I liked reading about you and your job. I just realized that it was probably your firm that does the bookkeeping and payroll for Silver Diamond Builders, where I worked with Steve. I know they outsourced all their accounting functions, and I recall Steve saying the firm they used was where his brother worked. Is that where you work? Do you work with Steve's brother? If so, I think that it's so weird that we've been adjacent to each other for so many years but had never met. I wonder if we ever would have, had you not taken Charlie? So, you're probably reading this on Labor Day. I know you went swimming at Michelle's yesterday. What are you doing today? If I were home, I'd be working all weekend or on call. The holiday pay is awesome, and I never pass it up. For now, I like my job too, not sure what else I'd do. Your statement of what you would do if you won the lottery got me thinking. I'd probably quit my job and volunteer at Animal House too. LOL though, I'd probably bring home a lot of dogs. I think the city ordinance limits me to a maximum of five dogs, and I'm sure I would hit the limit. Charlie would love to have that many brothers and sisters. I'd also volunteer my time working with kids, most likely at-risk youth. A friend's wife teaches summer kids camps revolving around arts and crafts at different places through the summer, churches, junior colleges, and park districts. I could see myself doing that with survival-type courses, or even just sports camps. Oh, to dream.

And speaking of dreaming, I better get to it. More tomorrow,

Alex

Virginia

Maeve finished her beer as the server cleared their glasses and the baskets that had the remnants of the dinners they'd enjoyed. She'd had a burger and fries. She sat in the outdoor area of The Sports Spot with Steve Mills, his ex-wife Jill, and a group of Steve's friends, most of whom she knew. Steve had just ordered another round of drinks for everyone. If Maeve drank too much more, she'd be Ubering home. The band was setting up their equipment in the area that was designated for them, and one of the servers was just lighting the bonfire. It would be dark in less than an hour.

"They should have had the band on Friday or Saturday night," Jill said, checking her watch. "I have to get home for the babysitter in just over two hours. It may be Labor Day but it is a school night."

"They did have other bands all weekend. This band was booked, playing other venues in Norfolk on Friday, Saturday, and Sunday," Steve said. "They're good; you'll like them. We'll be able to stay for their first set."

"You don't have to leave just because I do, Steve," Jill said.

He took hold of her hand, in her lap. "I want to come home with you and prove that you and the kids come before anything else."

Jill smiled and nodded.

Maeve was impressed with how Steve handled that. He really was trying to be a different partner and father than he had been the first time around. Even Maeve knew that Steve had not been the best husband and father before the divorce. His sports and teams often came before the family. He didn't sacrifice his playtime for family time. Jill felt resentment that she was the only one putting the family first, and that was the beginning of the end of their family.

"Oh my God! She has a lot of nerve, showing her face here," Jill suddenly said. She nodded to a group of tables on the far side of the outdoor area, well out of hearing range.

Maeve's eyes followed hers. She didn't recognize anyone at those tables. She glanced back at Jill and Steve. "Who?"

"Ashley Renner," Jill said.

Steve shook his head at his ex-wife, a silent warning. "Babe, I didn't tell you; Maeve is fostering Alex Richmond's dog, Charlie, while he's deployed. They've been writing emails to each other and getting acquainted. They'd be good together, don't you think?"

Jill's facial expression was one of guilt. "Oh my God, really?"

"Yes, it's a small world. I've never met him, but we discovered multiple points of overlap in our lives, like us both knowing Steve. Why the reaction? And who is Ashley Renner?" Maeve asked.

"Oh, crap, I'm sorry." Jill turned to Steve and said under her breath, "I wish you'd told me before."

But Maeve heard her. "Why? What's up, guys?"

Steve leaned over towards Maeve. "Remember I told you Alex's ex-girlfriend didn't like dogs, and he had to choose? Well, Ashley, the blond at the far high-top table over there up against the fence is the ex-girlfriend. And Jill is right. She has a lot of nerve showing up here.

She was nasty to us after they broke up. We haven't talked to her since, but she knows this is our hangout."

Maeve glanced over and saw who he must have been talking about. She was a walking Barbie doll. She was gorgeous with long blond hair, a thin and shapely body with perfect breasts, a perfect smile, a perfect glowing tanned complexion, and hanging on the arm of a perfect Ken doll. "That's Alex's ex-girlfriend?"

"Yes, a total piece of work. Don't let that pretty face fool you. She's a very ugly person inside once you get to know her. She hid who she really was from Alex and the rest of us for a long time," Steve said.

"I'm just glad Alex figured her out and ended it," Jill said.

Maeve's gaze hadn't left the woman they talked about. Ashley Renner. She'd remember that name. She planned to look her up on social media later. Maeve couldn't believe that gorgeous woman was Alex's ex-girlfriend. And even worse, Maeve was nothing like her. If that woman was Alex's type, she surely was not.

"Maeve," Jill's voice cut in on her thoughts. "You're so much more likable than she is. And don't judge Alex too harshly for going out with someone like her. As Steve said, she hid how much of a shallow bitch she was for a long time."

Maeve re-affixed her gaze on Jill. "I wouldn't judge Alex. I don't really even know him." She forced a chuckle. "Who he's gone out with in the past is his business."

"You've been emailing with him for several months," Steve said. "You know him pretty well by now. With Alex, what you see is what you get."

"Yeah, he seems like a nice guy," Maeve said, hoping to put this conversation to bed. "So tell me more about this band, Steve."

Steve gratefully let the subject be changed. He wished he had told Jill about Alex and Maeve getting to know each other, but there hadn't been a reason to mention it. Who would have predicted Ashley would be here tonight?

While Maeve had a fun evening, dancing and laughing with the group, she couldn't keep her eyes off Alex's ex. Maeve was never the jealous type, and really what would she be jealous of? They weren't together, and from what Steve and Jill had said, it sounded as though it had ended badly. But she was curious about the woman.

Maeve stayed for about an hour after Steve and Jill left. She had a good time and was glad she'd gone. The band was good, as Steve had said. She'd go see them again, provided Ashley Renner wasn't a groupie that followed the band. She really didn't want to see that woman again.

Arriving home, Charlie greeted her with his normal tail wags and nuzzles. After letting him out for the last time, and ensuring the house was locked up, she settled in bed and brought up her Facebook app to search for Ashley Renner. She found her easily enough. Her profile picture was of her wearing a crown.

She scrolled through her posts. There were a lot of them. "Your master really liked her? I'm not sure how," she said aloud to Charlie, who lay next to her. "Everything I see on her page looks fake."

Charlie stretched and rested his head in her lap.

Further down, she saw something that stopped her dead in her scrolling. Ashley Renner had been Miss Virginia in her early twenties. "Seriously? I shouldn't be surprised she competed in beauty pageants." she said to Charlie.

She petted him as she continued to scroll through Ashley's posts and pictures. "She sure likes to take selfies," she remarked after scrolling for over ten minutes. After a few more minutes, she exited Ashley's page. She'd learned enough about the woman. She was an esthetician at a high-end spa in Norfolk. In every picture she posted, she was dressed to the nines, and her hair and makeup were done to perfection, as they had been that night. She appeared to be a very superficial person who valued appearances. There was very little substance posted by her. And what was there didn't seem genuine, like her praise of her boyfriend, the Ken doll she was with at The Sports Spot. It was too showy, bordering on gross.

Maeve had to wonder if she'd posted that kind of kissy-face praise of Alex when they were going out. There was nothing on her page that led anyone to think she even knew him, not even a picture of Alex in a group. She'd purged it all, which led Maeve to believe it had been a bad breakup. That was what she'd done to her social media accounts too, purged anything with Michael in it.

Posting all that gross praise of her boyfriend was nothing that Maeve would ever be comfortable doing, nor would she be happy having someone post about her. She shook it off, almost wishing she didn't know about Ashley Renner.

She turned her bedside light off and snuggled Charlie. It was late, and she had work the next day. Jill was right about that; it was a school and work night for most. Labor Day Monday was not the night to be out late.

Just before lunchtime, Maeve checked her email for a message from Alex. She was disappointed that there wasn't one. She had her picture of Charlie ready to go, a shot of him in bed with the covers over him. His head was on the pillow. The caption she'd put on it was *I don't want to get up in the morning after the holiday weekend*. She tapped out a quick, short email.

Hi Alex,

I stayed out a bit too late last night, slept in, and am playing catch-up at work. Hope you had a good day.

Maeve

Later that afternoon, she went to the post office to mail the box of cookies she'd made. She'd stopped on the way and also purchased some candy bars and sunflower seeds, which she slipped into the box before taping it closed. If she had any idea of what types of magazines he might like, she would have put a few in as well.

Africa

Alex stretched out on his bunk and opened his email. That same feeling of happiness skipped through him at seeing her name in the list of new emails. He was a bit disappointed by the short email, and he wondered who she had been out with, not that it was his business. At that thought, he had an internal dialogue with himself. He called himself an idiot, trying to tell himself he wasn't interested in Maeve. He knew he was. He also realized that he'd never asked Maeve if she was seeing someone. He'd just assumed she wasn't as in all their email conversations she'd never mentioned a partner.

He thought about how to ask without asking as he looked at Charlie's picture. He chuckled at seeing him in bed. He'd noticed her bed before, the lavender comforter and the floral sheets. So, based on the colors, it was unlikely a guy lived with her. That was something at least. But that didn't mean she wasn't seeing someone.

Hi Maeve,

I can honestly say I don't have those days here. Hope you had a good time. Let me live through you. Can you tell me what you did over the Labor Day weekend? Charlie looks pretty comfortable. If it were me, I wouldn't want to get up either.

Talk to you later.

Alex

He read it again before he sent it. It didn't sound too nosy, was mildly suggestive in a flirty fun way, not in an obnoxious way, or at least he hoped that was how it would come across to her. He hit send. Then, he put his phone on the charger and settled in for the night. Operations were ramping up, and he had to be up early for the expanded grid they would be searching the next day.

***

The emails continued daily, and they discussed many different topics. Most of the pictures Maeve sent were of her and Charlie, which he loved. He came back one day in the middle of September from patrol to find a box on his bunk. The return address was Maeve Torres, with her address. He'd look it up later on Google Earth to look at where she lived. He didn't know the street. He opened the box and, seeing what was inside, his heart swelled in his chest. Wow. She baked his favorite cookies. That had to be the most thoughtful thing anyone had ever done for him.

"What do you have there?" Darren asked, coming up beside him. "Oh, Snickers, can I have one? And are those home-baked cookies?"

Alex held the box up, offering him one as he put one into his own mouth. It was delicious.

"Did your mom make them?" Darren asked, chewing the cookie and grabbing a Snickers bar.

"No, Maeve did," Alex said, still stunned that she had.

"Damn, Alex, I hope you like this girl. She's obviously got it for you."

"It's just a box of cookies," Alex said.

"She took the time to make them and take them to the post office to mail them. She wouldn't do that for someone she wasn't interested in. It's not just a box of cookies, dude."

"I'm not going to read anything else into it," Alex said. "All I'll say is that it was very nice of her."

"No wonder you're single; you wouldn't know if a woman was interested in you even if she baked you your favorite cookies."

Alex laughed as he took a bite of the cookie. Darren raised his own cell phone and took a picture of Alex.

"What are you doing?" Alex asked, still laughing.

"You've got to send her a picture of you enjoying the cookies. Trust me on this one," Darren said.

Alex's text message chime sounded.

"There, I sent it to you. Send it to her with a thank you."

"I'll think about it," Alex said as he devoured another cookie.

Darren grabbed his phone out of his hand and searched Alex's contacts. He attached the picture to a text to Maeve and hit send. "Decision made. I just sent it for you." He handed the phone back to Alex.

Two of the other guys came over to see what was in the box. They helped themselves to some of the goodies.

Virginia

Maeve's afternoon was going slowly. She'd finished the most complicated client files and had two files left that were always a breeze. She'd be done early with her workday. Charlie lay on the couch taking a nap. She'd take him out for a walk when she was done working.

Her text message chime brought her attention to her phone. The preview had a picture. Her heart did a little flip in her chest, and she felt her smile broaden over her face as she gazed at Alex's smile, one of her cookies in his hand at his mouth. A second text popped in beneath the photo.

> This is the nicest thing anyone has ever done for me, and the most delicious. Maeve, thank you

so much.

Her gaze went again to his picture. His hair was longer than in the pictures on his Facebook page, and he hadn't shaved in a while. His bright blue eyes twinkled, a stark contrast to the black hair on his head and on his face. He wore a desert camouflage shirt, with the sleeves rolled up. She saw an army-green wall behind him. It was kind of startling to see, a reminder that he really was in the military and deployed. She wasn't sure what image of him had been in her mind's eye when she thought about him, but it wasn't this.

Then the realization hit her that he had texted, not emailed. She chuckled, remembering that he didn't know how to attach a picture to an email, just a text message. She hit reply to message him back.

You're very welcome. I hope the recipe I found makes them close to what you're used to. I nibbled on a few, just to taste-test them, mind you, LOL. I thought they were good.

Yes, very good. Again, Maeve, thank you for them and the other goodies in the box. You made my day. Though a couple of my friends are raiding the box as I type this text out so I won't get to enjoy all of it myself.

Maeve laughed reading his text. She felt proud that he liked the gesture. It felt good to send him a little piece of home and make his day.

Enjoy! I was happy to send it.

October

Virginia

With Halloween in three weeks, Maeve put up her decorations on the front of the house. Decorating for the holidays was one of her favorite things to do, and she decorated for all of them. She had bins of her decorations organized on shelves in the garage. That was one benefit of living alone with a two-car garage. There was plenty of space to store things on the vacant side. There were a lot of preschool and school-aged children in her neighborhood, and she normally had a lot of trick-or-treaters. She was sure Charlie would do well with them.

On the top of one of the bins were the costumes she dressed her dogs up in. Holding the costumes, she felt weepy. She wouldn't have guessed last year when she got these costumes from the bin that it would have been the last time both of them would have worn them. She glanced over at Charlie. This would be the only Halloween Charlie would be here for. When Alex returned, he'd go home.

She couldn't stop the sadness that filled her, nor could she stop the tears that spilled from her eyes. "Well, that hit from nowhere," she told Charlie. She leaned down and gave him a hug. "What do you say? Lion or vampire?" She held both costumes up in front of him. He nosed the lion costume. "Good choice," she said.

She put the vampire costume away in the bin and then finished putting up the outside decorations. She put the lion costume on Charlie and had him sit on the front porch. She took several pictures from both at a distance and close up. She'd send a few to Alex later.

After the text messages about the cookies, they'd gone back to emailing. She assumed that there was a reason he preferred emailing to texting, which was odd to her, but she followed his lead. She wouldn't mind more texting. It was closer to a conversation.

She brought Charlie back inside and settled into her desk chair with the intention of putting in at least four hours on her client files. But first, she drafted an email to Alex.

> So today, Charlie and I put the Halloween decorations up. I have several dog costumes, and I let Charlie pick which he wanted to wear. LOL, he makes a great lion! I have to buy my Halloween candy, as we normally get a lot of trick-or-treaters in my neighborhood. Did you get many at your place? If you were home, would you have done anything special for Halloween? I'm just curious if we would have ended up at the same Halloween party either at someone's house or at a bar or maybe at The Sports Spot. Steve and Jill are trying to put together a group to go to The Sports Spot's Halloween party. Did you know they are kind of back together? I was out with them one night over Labor Day weekend, and they were good. I hope it works for them.

More later,

Maeve

Africa

"Back together?" Alex said aloud when reading Maeve's most recent email.

Steve and Jill were back together? How did that happen? He wondered. He had been surprised when they had separated and even more surprised when they went through with the divorce. He'd thought the time apart during their separation would have slapped them both in the face as to what a divorce would mean to their young family.

But it didn't.

Jill had easily picked up the slack at home and discovered she didn't need Steve, and Steve got used to not having to be there to help and filled his time with sports and the other things he loved with his friends. That's what it had looked like from Alex's point of view, anyway. Steve had been selfish, trying to hold on to the freedom of his single life, which had caused a lot of the problems to begin with. Even Alex could see that. Not that Jill was innocent in the demise of their marriage. She took every time Steve did anything with his friends as a personal affront after they'd had kids.

Alex's mother had suggested that Jill was jealous that she didn't have the same freedom to go out because her friends didn't get out without their babies that much. Most of them also had young children. Or that she wasn't coping well with the demands of being a parent, which usually fell more on a mother's shoulders. But Alex also saw that Steve and Jill had stopped talking and sharing what they wanted and appreciated in each other. Jill would get mad and say, "Fine, just go with your friends." And Steve would do just that.

Their relationship taught Alex a lot about what not to do. Of course, that didn't help him at all when his relationship with Ashley went to shit, or more accurately, when she showed her true colors and he was blindsided to learn what kind of person she was. And to think he was planning to ask her to marry him. She never would have baked him cookies, but then again, she wouldn't have stuck around and waited while he was deployed. Her ego constantly had to be fed, which he couldn't have done from Africa.

Alex opened the pictures in the email, his mood instantly changing, and he nearly laughed out loud at Charlie dressed up as a lion. Why hadn't he ever thought of dressing Charlie in a costume for Halloween? And he was never one to decorate his house for any holiday, but her decorations did bring a smile to his face. He remembered that his mom used to decorate like that every holiday. He remembered that vividly. He wondered whether his mother decorated their place in Florida. He'd never asked.

He re-read Maeve's email and figured out that over Labor Day weekend when she'd been out late, she probably had been out with Steve and Jill. For some reason, that thought made him feel better, not that there couldn't have been some guy there with her too or that she didn't hook up with another friend of Steve's.

Hi Maeve,

I can't believe that Steve and Jill are back together. I mean, if they can reconcile and forgive each other for everything in the past and move forward, that's great. I just know most people can't do that. And if I was home and Steve invited me, yes, I would come to a Halloween party. And I would have subbed in for volleyball over the summer too, so I would have seen you then. I'd like to think that if we'd met randomly that we would have hit it off. So, I actually just considered removing that part about hitting it off, but decided to leave it in. I really feel like we've become friends, and I think we would have even if we'd met by chance. And dare I say, I am looking forward to meeting you in person. By the way, your Halloween decorations look great, and Charlie, LOL, he makes the best lion!

Alex

Virginia

A warm feeling filled Maeve reading Alex's email where he said that he thought they'd hit it off if they met randomly and that he was looking forward to meeting her in person. So, he did plan to meet her. Would they have some sort of relationship? Friends? More? Although she too was looking forward to meeting him in person, a part of her dreaded that day, because she knew that when he returned, she would have to give Charlie back to him. And she had become quite attached to Charlie.

Not one to normally look at the downside of anything, Maeve suddenly felt sad and sunk into negative feelings. The last year had been really shitty.

First, she found out that Michael was a cheat, and she broke off the engagement so close to the wedding. It had been embarrassing having to call her parents and brother to tell them it was off, cancel your work vacation time, and then she had to tell everyone else. Not to be petty or paint herself as the victim, but she did tell everyone of Michael's betrayal. Okay, it did feel kind of good getting revenge by telling everyone on the guest list that she had walked in to find him in bed with another woman. And even though her logical brain told her it was all on him and it wasn't her fault, she was good enough, self-doubt crept in. Was she so unattractive or boring in bed he went elsewhere for it? And then, of course, the self-doubt about whether she could ever trust her instincts again when it came to men. Next came worrying about STDs until several tests came back clean.

She was just pulling herself out of that dark, angry and hurt place when Beatrix fell ill. Tests revealed heart failure, and the medication never helped her bounce back. A month later, Potter suffered what had to have been a stroke. The vet tried several medications, but within a week, Potter died. A few weeks after that, Beatrix also crossed over the Rainbow Bridge.

Yeah, a really shitty few months.

Maeve tried her best to shake off the unpleasant mood she'd dropped into. Once she'd finished her work, she changed her clothes, and she took Charlie with her for a run. A little time of the feet pounding the pavement would help get her out of her funk, she was sure. Running was one thing that had helped her during the previous shitty year. There was nothing like the flood of endorphins, serotonin, and dopamine she got when she went for a long run. The sunshine and fresh air helped as well.

Charlie was a great running buddy. By the time they returned to her house, she felt better. After a nice long shower, she felt like a new person. After she fed Charlie dinner, she made herself a healthy Cobb salad. Instead of turning the television on, she grabbed her Kindle and opened a new book she'd downloaded, a Hallmark-style feel-good romance. Michelle had recommended it.

As she settled into bed that night, she remembered she hadn't emailed Alex back that afternoon when she'd received his email. She re-read it, thought about it, and then tapped out a reply.

Hi Alex,

Yes, I have to agree. I think we would have hit it off if we'd randomly met when we were both single. I was in a relationship last summer, which is probably why I don't remember you at volleyball. I, too, feel we've become friends. I enjoy our email conversations. I'm looking forward to actually meeting you in person too. I'm sure you are anxious to get home and see Charlie. I'm glad I fostered him.

More tomorrow,

Maeve

Africa

Just as seeing Maeve's name in the email list gave Alex a jolt of excitement, not seeing it left him feeling disappointed. And that night was no exception. Alex was saddened when he opened his email and there was no reply from Maeve. He thought about what he'd written in his last email. Had his declaration that he felt as though they were friends, and he looked forward to meeting her, freaked her out? He had hesitated for a moment after writing it, second-guessing whether he should delete it, but he decided he had to put it out there.

It had been four months that they had been writing to each other. There was more going on between them than just her fostering Charlie and letting him know Charlie was doing well. Alex knew he was emotionally involved with her and that he was attracted to her. He had developed real feelings for her as a person, as a woman. And they were not platonic feelings.

He was sure a shrink would have a field day with him, developing feelings for a woman he'd never met, who wrote to him when he was deployed to an isolated hellhole. He was sure the shrink would tell him he was feeling dependent on her because she provided an escape from his job there. And that it wasn't real and couldn't be lasting.

But he knew how he felt; his feelings were real. He believed it could be lasting, a relationship with her. She was the type of person he would be friends with, and weren't the best and most enduring relationships born out of friendship? At least with it starting this way, he believed who she showed herself to be was genuine. She wasn't trying to be someone she wasn't to keep a romantic relationship going.

He hoped she'd just been busy and unable to write. It would be shitty if she hadn't, because his last email put her off somehow. He decided to just go ahead and email her, like he normally would.

Hi Maeve,

Hope you had a good day today. I was out in a slightly different search grid today for about ten hours. The weather here was really hot today. I have to say it was very unpleasant. It's dry and dusty, and I was thinking the leaves on the trees back home have to be changing color by now. I like fall and the fall colors. I even like raking leaves. There's a couple of red leaf maple trees in my yard, many up and down my street, and they are always so beautiful. You take it for granted when you're there seeing it, but trust me, when you're in such a parched and desolate landscape as I am right now, you miss it. And it makes you thankful for where you do live.

But what we're doing here is important. I'm reminded of that every day. This is a short time in the overall scheme of things that I'm here. We did get word that we're looking at returning home closer to the six-month mark rather than the nine-month max possibility we were given. That was great news to get today. Fingers crossed.

I'll let you go. Gotta get a shower and then hit the rack. Tomorrow's another day, and it's supposed to be even hotter tomorrow.

Alex

Virginia

Maeve checked her email and, in addition to seeing one in her inbox from Alex, she found the email she'd written the night before in her 'Drafts' folder. She'd never sent it. She felt bad about receiving the email from Alex, knowing she hadn't sent one early enough for him to see it before going to sleep the day before. She knew that where he was, it was seven to eight hours ahead of her time. She also knew he went to bed early as he got up very early to start his long day in the early morning hours to put in some time before it got too hot. So when she read his email, he'd just written it and sent it that day, but he didn't read her return email until the next night. Was that right? Was that how the time change affected things? She had to really think about it to figure it out.

First, she sent the draft email from the night before, making sure it went before anything else. Then she went outside and snapped a few pictures of the trees with the vibrant fall-colored leaves. He was right about that. The fall colors were beautiful. Knowing he'd be up for a short while yet, she texted the pictures to him, hopeful he'd see them.

Hey, I just found yesterday's email to you in my

drafts folder. I'm not sure how it didn't send, but I just hit send. Hope you get it before you go to bed. And yes, the fall colors are beautiful right now. This is the view from my front porch.

Then she opened her email and started a new message. Even though the news that he may be home sooner meant she'd have to give Charlie up sooner, she thought about it from his perspective. He was away from home in a desolate and unpleasant place, his own words. And he was excited about the news.

Alex,

Great news that you may be home sooner than originally thought. I'm sure you are anxious to get home. When people say, 'Thank you for your service,' they really have no clue what that service really is, or what sacrifice they make in their lives to serve their country. You just have Charlie, but I know many serving in active duty, in the reserves, and in the national guard have families. So, they're leaving their kids, missing birthdays, holidays, important milestones in addition to the day-to-day to go to unpleasant places like you're in. I guess I never really thought about it before. And believe me, I've been one to say to a veteran, 'Thank you for your service.' As odd as it is, I've only known a handful of military members as an adult. You'd think I would know many living this close to the base in Norfolk. I have one good friend from college that married a man in the Navy. That's it. Well, stay cool, my friend, or as cool as you can.

Maeve

She quickly hit send, hoping he'd see this email too.

Africa

The cool shower was refreshing. The showers were in a different building. He crossed the compound back to his quarters and entered to find many of his roommates already asleep on their bunks. Darren was still awake. He sat on his bunk with his earbuds in, playing a game on his tablet. He knew that Darren was listening to music.

Alex threw him a head nod and then laid on his bunk. Out of habit, he picked up his phone from the little shelf beside the bed and saw the text from Maeve with the picture of the fall-colored leaves on the trees. That was so nice of her to go take the pic and text it to him. Reading her text regarding the email the night before not sending, he smiled and eagerly brought up his email.

He read her email, happy that his openness hadn't stopped her from writing back. He found it interesting that she specifically said had they not been in a relationship, they would have hit it off. He tried not to read more into that statement. It could be interpreted in several ways, though the most obvious would be a non-platonic interest would be there. He also noted that she'd said she was in a relationship last summer, which implied to him, just by its wording, that she wasn't in one now. Or maybe that was wishful thinking on his part. Yeah, he really needed to reach out to Steve Mills.

Then a second email from her popped in. He read it and smiled at how she said my friend. He was glad she felt the same way. He sent a quick email acknowledging receipt of both emails and said goodnight.

Their daily emails continued to keep him company throughout the remainder of October. Alex had forgotten the date until he opened his email one night to see Charlie in the lion costume sitting by a large orange pumpkin bowl of candy. The caption Maeve had on the photo was 'Meany Maeve won't let me have even one piece!' He laughed out loud. He checked his watch. It was Halloween. Opting to send a message she'd see right away, he opened his text message string with her.

> Happy Halloween! Charlie looks ready to greet the trick-or-treaters. And good call on being a meany; candy is not good for him. So the question is, are you dressed up too?

He wished he hadn't asked when another text popped in with a picture that sent a sudden rush of blood south. Maeve wearing a very sexy pirate costume.

> Well, shiver me timbers, and every other part of me. You are a stunning pirate wench.

> Wench nothing, I'm the pirate captain.

Alex laughed inside, a grin on his lips.

> Aye, aye, captain. I'd follow any of your orders.

> LOL I'd have you on my crew any day.

> Seriously, nice costume. That's right, you're going to a get-together Steve and Jill are hosting, right?

> Yes, it's at The Sports Spot. I wish you were going to be there.

She wished he'd be there. Alex's heart swelled in his chest, just as something else was swelling at the thought of seeing her in person in that outfit.

> You and me both. Say hi to Steve and Jill for me, will you?

> Of course. If you were going, what would you dress as?

Alex thought about what a good reply to that question would be. He wanted it to be kind of flirty but not obnoxiously so.

> The pirate's hostage, obviously.

> LOL, and if you didn't know what I was dressing up as?

> I'd contact Steve and ask what the nicest, prettiest, smartest, most interesting single woman at the party who loved dogs was dressing as. He'd of course say you were going to dress as a pirate, so my costume would be the same. And our commonality in costume choice would give me a segue to make striking up a conversation with you easy.

Alex smiled with satisfaction as he hit send. Then he waited for her response. This text message exchange had been fun. Even though he had been exhausted, he was now revived. He hoped she had more time to text before she had to leave for the Halloween party.

> What a calculated approach to picking your costume.

Alex banked on her statement being made in fun.

> Yes, ma'am. I'd do what I had to, to enable me to secure your attention at the costume party. And if there was a costume contest, we'd enter it together and win. LOL.

> I do like a man who sets goals and is methodical in achieving them.

> That is me.

Just then, the door to the barracks swung open, and the lights were turned on. The duty officer stood in the doorway. "Charlie Unit, you've been scrambled for a priority mission. Get your gear and meet in the briefing room in fifteen minutes. You'll head out from there."

Alex tapped out a quick text to Maeve.

> Sorry, I've just been scrambled. Have to go. I've enjoyed chatting. Have fun tonight and be safe. I'll be in contact when I can, not sure when that will be.

Virginia

Maeve enjoyed texting with Alex. It had been a fun, flirty exchange. She loved his response to her costume, which was what she had hoped for. And his description of her disguised as what he'd ask Steve, made her feel good. Did he really think those adjectives described her?

When his last text popped up on her phone, she felt sad. And worried about him. What exactly did scrambled mean? She assumed it to mean he was suddenly pulled from where he was to go some place that urgently needed his specialty, which, if that was the case, was bound to be dangerous.

> Yes, please text when you can. Be safe, Alex.

She didn't have time to dwell on his last text as trick-or-treaters began to ring her doorbell. She and Charlie handed out candy from four p.m. until six p.m., when it finally slowed down. The Halloween party started at seven. She knew there'd be appetizers there, but she ate a protein bar and downed a bottle of water before she let Charlie out for the last time before she left. She turned the television on in her bedroom and called him onto the bed. Then, she set the bowl of candy on her porch with a note asking each person to only take two pieces as trick-or-treating technically went until seven. She was sure the bowl would be empty when she returned.

The parking lot at The Sports Spot was already quite full of cars when she pulled in. She easily found Steve, Jill, and their group on the back patio, in their normal area. Steve hadn't been kidding when he'd said The Sports Spot was their hangout. She greeted them with hugs. "I was texting with Alex earlier, and he asked that I tell you hello from him."

"Texting, huh?" Steve said.

"Yes, I sent him a picture of Charlie in his Halloween costume," Maeve said.

Steve gave her a look that told her he didn't believe that was the extent of the exchange. But he didn't question her further. He just smiled. "That was nice of you. Here, put on this wristband. It'll let you grab food and drinks, and the bartender will put it on my tab." He slipped the orange bracelet onto her wrist and then pointed towards the bar.

"Thanks," Maeve said.

The evening turned out to be a lot of fun. Maeve knew most of the guests and enjoyed the party. She was glad she'd gone. After she was home and snuggled with Charlie in bed, she let her mind wander, envisioning what the night would have been like had Alex been there.

Her imagination came up with several scenarios, each of them including passionate kisses at her front door. In one version, she invited him in, and he stayed the night. Imaginary sex with him was incredible. In the conjured encounter where the night ended with intense kisses, exchanging phone numbers, a lengthy romance followed culminating in his surprise proposal, which she excitedly accepted. Cut to the wedding, a simple, private affair, and a happy life. Not all men were like Michael, as her friend Michelle had repeatedly said. In her fantasy, Alex was the perfect man, and she would get her happily ever after.

She laughed at herself and her musings, but inside, she knew that since she'd been able to let her imagination run wild and consider a relationship, she was inching closer to being ready for another one. Her heart was healing, and her guard was coming down.

November

Africa

A team of SEALs had called in EOD support. Alex and his teammates arrived in Djibouti in the early morning hours of November first. They were the closest unit to assist. From there, the Black Hawk chopper dropped them in Somalia just outside of the range from the perimeter of the target compound the SEALs were waiting to breach. It was believed to be heavily booby-trapped with IEDs. Inside the compound were the Somali pirates and hostages taken from the cargo vessel they'd attacked in the Gulf of Aden.

When sitting in the five-minute briefing pre-deployment, when the word pirate was used, the image of Maeve in her sexy pirate costume flashed through his thoughts. Before he had time to shake that image from his mind and appropriately replace it with a rail-thin Somali male, they loaded onto the plane that transported them to Djibouti.

He and the team had minimal sleep, just what they could grab while en route. On the ground, the team immediately got to work to clear a footpath of booby-traps that led up to the back of one of the buildings the SEALs had decided was their best entry point into the compound. They came across multiple buried explosives and a couple of tripwires connected to IEDs that would be fatal to anyone passing through.

The back of the building was rough-hewn wood, which looked to be the peeled bark from trees similar to those nearby. Alex knew with thin wood such as this, triggering devices could be easily disguised within the overlapping sections. He also examined a barbed wire fence with what looked to be detonation wire strung through it. The fence was connected to each of the buildings in the compound. The entire fence was booby-trapped. There was one main gate that was heavily guarded, and guards patrolled the compound.

The explosives sniffing dog, Victor, was brought in. He alerted on two sections of the wall, positive for explosives. Alex's team pointed out the clear sections and the SEALs breached in one corner that was clear. After they were inside and had ensured it was secure, Alex brought Victor in. After a thorough search, no further explosives were found. A drone with thermal imaging had completed a flyover just before Alex and his team arrived. It showed the heat signatures, the people, were clustered in one building which lay mostly kitty-corner to the building they'd just breached.

"We've got it from here," the SEAL commander told them. "Get back to your primary LZ for extraction and thanks for the assist."

Alex and his team left immediately. They carefully retraced their steps through the heavy brush and wooded area, which gave way to the desert grass where outcroppings of the rocky terrain strangely pushed free from the ground and sections of the sandy, parched earth intermingled with the dry desert grasses.

When they were less than a click from their primary extraction point, muffled shots and a single explosion were heard from the direction of the compound. Alex knew those sounds indicated the SEALs were engaging. He hoped they'd rescue the ship's crew that was being held for ransom without injuries or fatalities to the hostages or the SEAL team.

They picked up the pace to put more distance between themselves and the skirmish. When they were nearly to the primary LZ, Trejo, the team member at the front of the line, gave the hand signal that everyone needed to take cover and freeze. He didn't transmit through comms, which told Alex that he'd seen something that was so close by that he didn't speak for fear of being heard.

Immediately, each member of the team silently faded into the tall desert grass; their weapons held at the ready. Peering through the blades of grass, Alex caught sight of movement less than thirty yards away. They were moving quickly towards the compound. He held his breath and didn't move a muscle.

As they came closer, cutting across their path, he saw that it was a group of about a dozen rail-thin Somali men and boys. They were armed with what looked to be old AK-47s, wearing tattered, ill-fitting clothes. A few didn't even have shoes on their feet. Although a definite threat, Alex felt a pang of pity for them. The poverty and starvation in this region of the world were horrendous. He wondered if they were reinforcements coming to aid those in the compound or if they were with a rival warlord who looked to capitalize on the downfall of another force and aid in their demise. More than likely, it would be their demise too.

He didn't worry about the SEALs. As their activities had been heard, they were already done at the compound and would have been out just as fast as they'd hit it, their exfil point to the south. The operation had been planned for maximum impact, to not only rescue the hostages but to disable the pirates by decimating the compound and its forces. They had explosives of their own that would have been planted all over the compound before they evacuated it. Tripping one charge would detonate the rest. Those men and boys who'd crossed their path would be blown up the second they stepped foot inside the compound.

And sure enough, just as Alex and his team reached the LZ and called in the bird for extraction, the deathblow to the compound resounded through the valley in the form of a series of rapid concussions, and thick black smoke billowed from the hillside where the compound had been located.

The Black Hawk landed, and the men climbed aboard. It pulled away as quickly as it had come in, gained altitude rapidly and sped away to bring them to safety. They landed at Camp Lemonnier in Djibouti and grabbed a hot meal. They were given overnight lodging in one of the barracks with running water, a five-star resort compared to their other accommodations. Following a hot shower, Alex stretched out on the bunk and turned his phone on.

He found two messages from Maeve with pictures of her and Charlie. That was home. That was normal. This last mission, this deployment, was no longer his normal, as it once had been. It was a realization that came to him and surprised him. Although he still had the training and the history of doing this job, and he still did it well, the drive and desire to do it were no longer the same as they once were.

He wanted to get home and play with his dog. He wanted to return to his job trimming trees. And he wanted to take the dark-haired beauty in the photos out on a date, spend time with her in person, and maybe start a relationship he wouldn't want to step away from for another deployment. He'd keep his feelings for her his little secret for now.

After a good night's sleep, they ate a good meal before they boarded their transport back to their own base. He hadn't messaged her back the night before as exhaustion overtook him. Her smile as she embraced Charlie was the last thing he saw before drifting off. It fueled some amazing dreams that night.

Virginia

Maeve felt relief when she opened her email to see Alex's name in the new email list. It had been a few days since he'd abruptly ended their fun conversation on Halloween. She'd been worried about him even though she tried not to be. She didn't know what his silence meant. Was it normal that he'd get scrambled and be out of touch? Well, he hadn't been in the five months they'd been communicating.

She opened the email and quickly read it.

Maeve,

Sorry, I had to be out of touch. I'm back at my regular base now. It was nice to see the messages from you waiting for me when I again could access my email. You don't know how much I appreciate you sending me pieces of home, pieces of normal life. Even just talking about dressing up for Halloween and telling me about the party is a piece of home and a nice distraction. And yes, in that sexy pirate costume, you were quite a distraction. So, keep the distractions coming. And cookies. Can I ask you to make me more cookies? Please?

Alex

She laughed out loud. It was great that he thought her Halloween costume was a sexy distraction. She wondered how many times over the past few days he had looked at the picture. And he wanted more cookies. That was something she could easily do for him.

She went to the store and bought the ingredients for the cookies that afternoon when she was done with work for the day. She also bought candy and other snack foods to put in the box as she knew he'd share whatever she sent with the other guys in his unit. Baking the cookies and packing the goodies in the box made her feel good. She knew that whatever she sent would be appreciated.

Africa

The worse day of Alex's deployment came during the second week of November. He was on patrol with his buddy, Darren and Victor, the explosive detection dog. They were clearing the structures in a village that had been liberated and was due for resettlement, their primary mission in the region.

Victor alerted, but Darren didn't react fast enough. In a split second, the two men went from laughing about something Darren had said to chaos. An explosion tore open the small mud brick dwelling. The dry grass thatched roof instantly caught on fire and burned completely within seconds.

When Alex pulled himself to his feet he found Darren with large open wounds down his left arm, from the shoulder to the tips of his fingers. Victor lay on top of him, bleeding out. Nothing could be done for Victor. He called in the injury and provided Darren with pain relief and with what first aid he could, a tourniquet wrapped around the upper arm at the shoulder, until the medics swarmed the scene.

In the end, he brought Victor's body back to their base, cradling the dog in his arms while crying his eyes out for him. He wished he could turn the clock back and prevent the detonation. Darren was just as good at his job as he was. It easily could have been him on that side of the structure.

When he returned to his bunk, all he wanted to do was curl up into a ball and zone out for ten or twelve hours. Out of habit, he checked his phone. A message from Maeve waited. Tonight, she had a video attached of Charlie playing in the yard. She turned the camera towards herself and waved. Her smile was beautiful, bringing him a degree of peace. The last clip had Charlie dressed up like a pilgrim. Despite his incredible sadness, his lips tipped into a grin. Seeing the video of Charlie was just what he'd needed.

> Hi Maeve, I hope you're not too busy working to chat. I kind of need it right now. I had a shitty day. Seeing Charlie was just what I needed.

The text message chime was a welcome sound.

> Hi, yes, I have time. Why was your day shitty?

> I can't mention specifics, sorry. But tell me about your day.

He lay on his bunk in the darkness and messaged with her for over an hour. They talked about Charlie, the upcoming Thanksgiving holiday, the weather. Everything except for how horrible his day had been.

Virginia

Maeve enjoyed the texts with Alex as she worked from her home office. Charlie lay on the couch across from her desk. "I'm texting with your daddy," she told him. Even though she enjoyed the exchange, she had to wonder what was wrong.

> I should probably let you get back to work," Alex messaged.

> I've been working while we text. You're not interrupting me. I should let you get to bed, huh? It has to be late there.

> I'm lying in my rack, just not ready to sleep yet, I guess. I appreciate you keeping me company tonight.

> Of course. You know I enjoy chatting with you.

> I've appreciated your messages every day. Checking for your messages is the high point of my day.

A smile came to Maeve's face.

> Well, I know you miss Charlie.

She'd like to think that it was more than just seeing Charlie or hearing about his day that made Alex say that. She hoped he felt for her the way she had come to think of him. She, too, looked forward to his emails and texts.

Africa

Alex stared at her last text message for several long moments, deciding what his reply should be. Yes, of course, seeing Charlie and being assured he was being loved and cared for was the primary reason for looking forward to the daily emails from her. But he knew it was more than that.

Should he admit to his feelings regarding her? He enjoyed getting to know her. From what he'd learned about her; she was someone he wanted to get to know a lot better. How could he say that without making her feel uncomfortable? And he didn't want to freak her out by telling her that when she was in the photos or when she narrated content on a video, and he heard her voice, that his pulse quickened. He'd sound like some crazed stalker.

> Are you there?

She messaged after a few minutes with no reply.

> Yes, sorry, someone came in and asked me something.

He lied. He made a quick decision.

> I'm back now. Yes, your daily messages with pictures and videos help me not miss Charlie as much, but it's more than that. You know that I've enjoyed getting to know you and I already consider us friends. I really like talking to you

daily.

Maeve felt her smile spread.

After you're back, would you like to maybe get together sometime?

After she sent it, she felt the need to add to it, so it wouldn't sound like she was asking him out.

We seem to like to do a lot of the same things. Maybe we can do some of them together.

He replied before she even sent the last two sentences in the separate message.

I'd like that.

I'm doing a 5K at the end of January. If you're back by then, we could run it together.

I'm not sure of my return date yet, but that would be cool if we did.

I've also signed up for the Shamrock Shuffle again in March. Have you registered for it yet?

I'll have to do that. Can you send me the link?

He knew he'd be home in time for that 5K.

I've toyed with doing a half-marathon. Any interest? After you're back, we could train togeth-

> er. There are a few people in my running club
> thinking about it.

He had run several half-marathons. He would gladly do another with her and help her train for it. He also wanted to run a full marathon and then train for a triathlon. That was his ultimate fitness goal, to be in good enough shape to do a triathlon.

He loved that Maeve was so active. Ashley was not. And anything they did, she had to be one hundred percent dolled up, hair, makeup, and her clothes were always just perfect. He recalled how much that had bothered him at the time. It made her completely unspontaneous. Once he wanted her to go out to breakfast with him after they'd just woken up. It took her an hour to get ready. He wanted her to just throw her hair up into a messy bun or a ponytail and go. She couldn't do that.

Thinking back now, he wasn't sure how he hadn't seen how different they were at the time. Well, yes, he did know how he hadn't seen it. Ashley pretended to like everything he did. She made plans to do things with him, like run a 5K, and then she backed out at the last minute, feigning an injury or illness. Ashley hadn't been the only long-term relationship he'd had since he'd separated from active duty, but she had been in his life longer than the others. And the end of the relationship had been very contentious. With the other women he'd dated, he'd remained friends when their relationship had run its course.

After that night, all their communication was through text messages. Most nights he lay in his rack, messaging with her for hours. She was always available to chat, which he appreciated, especially because Darren had been flown to the U.S. hospital in Germany. From there, they would ship him stateside. His injuries were severe, and he would not be returning to the unit. Alex had gotten word that they weren't sure they could save his arm.

Virginia

She restructured her workday to accommodate their daily text messages, which usually went on for well over an hour until he would say that he was exhausted and had to go to sleep. And most photos of Charlie she sent thereafter included her in the frame. She liked that he also sent pictures of himself. In their conversations, they discussed anything and everything, and she continued to like the person she was getting to know.

She made him another batch of cookies, Thanksgiving-themed, which he repeatedly thanked her for. And the pictures he sent of him and several of his friends devouring them made her smile. It felt good to be appreciated, knowing she made a difference in their lives with something as little as a box of treats.

On Thanksgiving, she went to a potluck dinner at Animal House. Many of the other volunteers had no family to spend the holiday with either. It was dinner for twelve people, and Maeve brought one of the two stuffed turkeys they had. Everyone brought something to contribute to the meal, be it a side dish, a dessert, or paper plates, napkins, and plastic cutlery. One volunteer made dog cookies, which were enjoyed by all the shelter dogs. Maeve even brought a few home for Charlie.

There were many veterans who volunteered at the shelter; more than a few of them were disabled from their service. She knew a few of them well and, for the first time, she talked with them about Alex and his deployment during dinner. They knew what an EOD tech was and knew how dangerous the job was.

"I was a canine handler and did some work with an EOD unit,"

Miles, one of the veterans, said. Miles had scars on his hands, arms and even his head from burns. Maeve had heard that he'd been injured when the car he was traveling in hit an IED. "Those guys are highly trained, but you're right; the work is dangerous. How long have you been seeing him?"

"Well, I haven't actually been seeing him. I'm fostering his dog, so I've been writing and texting with him. He deployed in June."

"Ah, a long-distance relationship," Trevor Ferguson said. Trevor was another disabled vet who volunteered at the shelter. He had a prosthetic left arm. Seated beside Trevor was Julia. She was kind of the second in charge at Animal House.

"Why is this the first time we're hearing about this long-distance friend of yours, Maeve?" Julia asked with a suggestive smile.

Maeve laughed. "It's not exactly like that. I don't know exactly what we are besides friends. But we have definitely become friends since we've been writing to each other, and I've sent him pictures of Charlie."

"Well, you can believe that you're important to him," Trevor said. "You represent home and normal to him, two things he's really missing."

The other veterans chimed in with stories of their past deployments and what was most appreciated from home while they were away. It gave her a different perspective on being deployed.

After dinner, they took the dogs out into the play yards and played with them for a long time. Several hours later they put them back in their kennels. Miles was the overnight volunteer. He usually kept one or two of the dogs in the office with him when he did an overnight shift.

"Try to get that guy to come volunteer after he's back. It will help him if he has any PTSD at all," Miles told Maeve while giving her a hug at the end of the evening.

"I'll do that, thanks Miles."

He locked the door after everyone left the building. In the parking lot they exchanged hugs. It had been a fun way to spend the holiday, and Maeve would say that it was her favorite Thanksgiving dinner ever.

December

Virginia

The new text message chime sounded on Maeve's phone. She sat at her desk working on a customer's payroll taxes. She lifted her phone and read the message from Alex.

> I think my unit will be home by the New Year.

> That's great!

> Maybe even earlier.

> Even better for you. When will you know for sure?

> A few weeks. I'll let you know when I can.

Maeve took a deep breath, her gaze shifting to Charlie on the couch where he slept. She knew that she and Alex would at least be friends, so she'd still get to see him. But not having him around every day, she would miss him horribly. She loved him and was attached to him, even though she had told herself daily that he was someone else's dog that she had to give back. She was not cut out for fostering dogs. Her next one had to be an adoption. She could never do this again. The thought of giving Charlie back to Alex hurt her heart.

Here's the link to sign up for that 5K at the end of January, if you want to run it with me.

Great, yeah, thanks. I will sign up. It's a date!

Maeve smiled, seeing his words. Even though she knew it would be here before she knew it, the end of January still felt so far away.

A week later, he messaged that he might be home sooner than that. He couldn't give any details, though, due to operational security. As she put up her Christmas tree, she wondered if that meant before Christmas. She was planning to make him a batch of cookies after the tree was up. She decided to hold off. She didn't want to send him a package if he would be on his way home.

On Sunday morning, she decorated the backyard with lights strung on her fence and on her bushes and trees. She even strung lights on the small greenhouse that was in her backyard. After lunch, she took Charlie for a run, still training for the 5K that was just over a month away. The temperature was mild, in the low forties, but snow was due overnight. She was excited about the prospect of snow. Though with it falling this early, it would surely melt before Christmas.

Maeve stopped off at the Hounds and Grounds coffee shop, her run taking her right by it. She got a pup cup for Charlie and a hot salted caramel latte for herself. She'd had a good run, and now she'd walk home for the cooldown portion. While Charlie dug in, she snapped a few pictures of him to send to Alex. Charlie finished his treat, and they set out for home, the pace moderate.

As they rounded the corner and her house came into view, so did the old red pickup truck and the dark-haired man who stood beside it. She knew he could be none other than Alex Richmond. Even at this distance, she recognized him immediately. Her heart beat hard in her chest as though she was still racing at full speed. She picked up her pace, which, with the cup of coffee in her hand, she knew had to look ridiculous.

Alex smiled and waved when he saw Maeve and Charlie approaching. His heart warmed in his chest and his heartrate increased. He wasn't sure if he was more excited to see Charlie or Maeve. It had to be a tie. He'd felt exhausted from the full day of travel, and he'd been so disappointed that no one was home when he arrived at her house but seeing them both instantly revived him. He moved towards them.

When they were only half a block apart, Maeve dropped the leash. "Go get him, Charlie," she said.

Charlie charged at him at full speed when Maeve dropped his leash. Alex kneeled down and took the full brunt of Charlie plowing into him. Wagging tail, licks, and Charlie's body up on his, he drank in the sensation of holding his boy as he stroked his soft fur.

Then his eyes met Maeve's gorgeous dark browns. He grabbed hold of the leash and stood to face the amazing woman who now stood before him. "Maeve, it's so nice to meet you in person."

Maeve's eyes were trapped within the sparkling blue depths that were Alex's eyes. His face wore a broad, genuine smile. "I'd recognize you anywhere, Alex. When did you get back?" It was awkward for a moment. Maeve wanted to embrace him. Should she offer her hand?

Alex stepped into her and solved the dilemma. He wrapped his arms around her and pressed a kiss to her forehead. Then he just held her for a moment as he answered her question. "We landed a few hours ago. I came right here. I wanted to surprise you."

Maeve reciprocated the embrace, enjoying the sensation of his arms holding her. "Well, you did. I am surprised." Then the reality that he was there, and he'd want to take Charlie home with him hit her. Her smile fell.

"I have a huge favor to ask you," he said. He pointed at her house. "Can we go inside?"

"Oh, sure! Yes, of course," she stammered, trying not to cry, already knowing saying goodbye to Charlie was going to hurt. And she'd miss the daily texting sessions with Alex.

Once in the living room, Alex detached Charlie from the leash. Charlie jumped onto the couch and nuzzled his head against Alex's hand. Alex glanced around the room. "Your house is nice. I noticed that in the pictures and videos, but in person it's very comfortable."

"Thank you," she said, waiting for him to say he'd get out of her way and take Charlie home. Her heart hurt. She needed more time to get ready to say goodbye to Charlie, and now that Alex stood in front of her, she wanted to spend more time with him.

"Well, the favor. I hate to ask this, but I have no place to go. The guy renting my house has a lease through the end of January, and he said he can't leave early. I can go to a hotel if I can find one that allows dogs, but I'll be returning to my regular job, and I can't leave Charlie alone in a hotel room all day while I'm working. Can he stay a while longer?"

Maeve let out the breath she hadn't realized she'd been holding and the pressure on her heart eased. "Of course he can," she assured him, a big grin coming to her face. "So, you're going to pay to stay in a hotel for six weeks? That's going to be expensive," she said.

Alex shrugged. "Yeah, probably. I don't have any friends that I would ask if I could stay at their place. Six weeks is a long time to impose on someone."

Maeve thought about it for only a second. "Yes, you do. You don't have to ask. I'm offering. We're friends, aren't we? And I do have a spare room."

"Maeve, that would be great!" He rushed forward and enveloped her in a hug. His hands held her tightly. He enjoyed the sensation of her body pulled snugly against his own. It was something he'd fantasized about, something he'd yearned for, for so long. "And it would be good for Charlie, too. Thank you," he said, pulling back enough to look her in the eyes.

Her gaze locked with his. The smile on her face was beautiful. She was beautiful, even more so in person than in her pictures. He kissed her forehead again. Then her cheek. She turned her face, and her lips brushed the corner of his. The contact surprised him and sent zingers throughout him.

Maeve stared into his beautiful blue eyes. She was frozen in the moment, startled by the physical feelings that washed through her at his touch and his light kisses on her face. Her hands gripped his biceps, holding him in place. Her heart thumped hard in her chest, and what she felt wasn't just physical. Emotionally, she felt a connection to this man. All the conversations with him over the past six months had created a closeness, a real and powerful affection. Though she did find him handsome, her attraction to him was not just from his appearance. It was from his personality, his sense of humor, who he was, and what he believed in.

"Is it possible to fall for someone you've never met?" she asked, her voice a whisper.

"Absolutely," he replied. "I fell for you months ago. And I'd like to think that from all our conversations we know each other better than many people who go to bed after a few dates." After he said it, he regretted the phrasing. How presumptuous of him to assume that they were going to bed! "I mean, those kisses, whew! Any further it goes will be amazing, I'm sure. No pressure." He paused, taking in the shocked look on her face. "What I'm trying to say is, I really like you, Maeve, and I want to get to know you better. I'm really attracted to the person that you are. You have a kind heart and an incredible sense of humor. I don't want you to think I was assuming anything, because I wasn't. Unfortunately, my inner thoughts came out unfiltered." He shrugged and flashed her a self-deprecating grin. "I'm a guy and you're a beautiful and sexy woman. Of course I'm thinking of that."

Maeve couldn't help but smile, letting him off the hook. She didn't feel sexy at the moment. Her sports bra was soaked with sweat. She hadn't even washed her face that morning, nor had she brushed her hair. She'd just piled it on top of her head in a messy bun. "I'm really attracted to you too," she admitted. "But I need to take this slow while we get to know each other better."

"I'll follow your lead." He pulled her into an embrace and caressed over her back. "For the past six months you were my lifeline, tethering me to normal life while I was in hell. You took amazing care of Charlie, and I will forever be grateful to you. I look forward to spending time with you and getting to know you better."

Maeve melted into him. She ran his words through her thoughts several times, evaluating them. "I don't want you to think you owe me anything. You don't. The truth is, I loved all the emails and text messages. I loved taking the pictures of Charlie and coming up with the captions. If you had taken him home today, I would not only miss him, but I'd miss communicating with you. I'm glad you'll be staying with me."

Without thinking, his lips claimed hers. Or maybe it was that they both had the idea, and their lips were drawn together. Either way, an open-mouth kiss, tongues exploring, just happened. It was slow, passionate, everything a first kiss should be.

Then Maeve remembered sensible things, like she was sweaty from her run. She hadn't shaved her legs in months. And no matter how incredible it felt to be making out with this man, who she knew she'd fallen for over long distance, he was still a stranger. Or was he? She had to take things slower. Or did she? The physical sensations his kisses and caresses brought her were incredible. Even now, her skin tingled where he touched. She wanted more. A lot more.

She pulled her lips from his, only then realizing that she was left dizzy, a high feeling fogging her brain from that kiss. She was flooded with oxytocin, dopamine, and serotonin — happy hormones. It had been the perfect kiss, and her body was reacting.

She stared into his eyes and saw openness and affection. For some reason, she trusted him more than she had anyone since Michael. "That was nice."

Alex had gotten lost in the kiss, in the taste of her; warm salted caramel from the coffee she'd just gotten from the coffee shop. He'd waited months to see her and embrace her. He'd fantasized about holding her and kissing her. The reality far surpassed any sensations he'd conjured. And that she eagerly returned his kisses was fantastic. "Yes, it was. It was like, wow, incredible."

She smiled shyly. She felt the same but wasn't as open to declare it that way. "I need to get that shower," she said. "I'll show you to the guest room, and you can get settled in. Make yourself at home. And help yourself to anything in the refrigerator or cabinets; we can work out groceries and the other costs of living together later. I'm sure it won't be an issue."

"I promise I'll pay my fair share," he said. He'd be more than fair. He didn't want her ever to regret extending the invitation to stay. "Okay, I'll just go out and get my bag. At some point, I'll need to do laundry."

"No problem. I have a washer and dryer."

"And I'll need to arrange to go over to my place and get some more of my clothes and things," he said. "I'll keep it to a minimum, so I don't bring too much."

"Really, it's okay." She led him to the guest room, which was the first door on the right down the short hallway off the living room. "It's small, but it should work for you. And all the drawers in the chest are empty. Half of the closet is empty too. I just store my coats and off-season clothes in it, which I can move if you need the space."

He gazed in. There was a queen-size bed, a nightstand, a tall chest of drawers, and a desk. The furniture looked identical to his bedroom furniture. "Ikea?"

She smiled and nodded. "It was cheap."

"Yes, I have the same furniture in my bedroom," he returned her smile. "I won't take up too much space, I promise. Don't feel you need to scrunch any of your things on my account. You should see the small conditions I lived in for the last six months." He paused and chuckled. "We were housed in basically a shipping container, and there were eight of us in there. The army calls them modular barracks. There wasn't much space allotted to each of us, and there wasn't any privacy. There wasn't even any running water. We had to go across the compound to a unit that had the showers, sinks, and toilets." He smiled a genuine smile. "Believe me, this is a huge upgrade."

"So, you were at an Army base?"

"Yes, a temporary one. Our mission was clearing villages in South Sudan of IEDs that had been liberated from insurgents for the resettling of the villagers who had fled during the violence."

She was surprised by the matter-of-fact way he'd just said it, like it was a perfectly normal thing everyone did. "Wow, that's incredible," she said. "I don't even know what to say to that."

Alex chuckled. "I get the same reaction from my family regarding my job."

"It's just so extraordinary. I mean, regular people don't do that kind of thing."

He laughed again. "Yes, we do. I consider myself a regular person."

She shook her head and smiled. "I think a lot of people would call you a hero."

"Nah, I'm not that. I'm just a guy with training and maybe not much sense because I volunteered for the job."

"I'm sure the people who want to move back to their homes, who you helped to do that think of you as a hero."

He felt his cheeks heat. "Maybe, but really, I don't think of it that way."

His humility impressed her. "So," she began, to change the subject. She pointed down the hallway. "Bathroom, it's all yours. I have one in my room, so feel free to leave your toothbrush, razor, whatever in there. Just keep it tidy as it is the guest bath for company."

"Yes, ma'am," he said with a smile.

"My office, and my bedroom," she said as she pointed at each door. "And that's the grand tour. Laundry is in the kitchen. Feel free to use it whenever you'd like."

"Thank you, really, for everything."

"You're welcome." They stood staring at each other in silence for a long moment. "I'm going to get in the shower."

"And if you don't mind, I think I'll lie down with Charlie after I get my bag. It was a long flight back, and the time change is brutal."

"I can only imagine."

"I'll set my alarm for two hours so I can start to get on the right time zone. Do you have any plans for dinner?" he asked.

"No. I was probably just going to have some soup or something."

"I'd like to buy you dinner."

"You don't have to do that," she said.

"I know I don't, but I'd like to. I'd actually like to go out for a good steak and a big baked potato with all the trimmings." And he knew right where he wanted to go, his favorite steakhouse.

She smiled again. "That sounds good. Yes, and thank you. Dinner would be nice."

"Okay, get your shower, and Charlie and I will take our nap."

He retrieved his pack from the truck. He had a pair of khaki pants that would work for dinner and a suitable shirt to wear; the few civilian clothes he'd brought with him on deployment besides jeans and a few t-shirts. He would need to go to his house and get some of his clothes as well as his work gear from the garage. He'd be back at work in a couple of days.

He lay on top of the comforter, and Charlie jumped up with him right away. The bed was comfortable and with Charlie snuggling up against him, he drifted off right away.

Maeve locked both her bedroom and bathroom doors. A girl couldn't be too careful. And even though they'd conversed through email and text message for six months, Alex Richmond was a stranger, or was he? In some ways, maybe. In others, not at all. But she'd still play it safe. She felt euphoric that he would be staying with her, which meant that Charlie would be staying with her.

Maeve heard Alex's alarm going off as she passed by the spare room door. She paused and listened at the door until it was silenced. She was in her bedroom, tidying up when Alex opened the door. Charlie trotted into her room to find her as Alex crossed the hallway and went into the hall bathroom.

She caught a glimpse of Alex wearing only his pants. His chest, abs, and arms were bare and were tanned, sculpted lean muscles. It was quite a sight! It made her self-conscious of every roll or bulge on her not as toned body. Her thoughts went to the Barbie doll he'd last dated. She, too, had very little body fat. But then Steve and Jill's words about Ashley Renner echoed through her thoughts. She may be pretty on the outside, but she is ugly inside, Maeve reminded herself. No, Maeve would not compare herself to anyone.

"The bed is very comfortable, and I love the showerhead in the bathroom," Alex told her, coming into the kitchen after he was dressed. His hair was towel-dried, but still damp. "I slept great and feel revived."

"That's good to hear," she said.

"It is amazing having a private shower again," he said and chuckled. "The little things."

She let her eyes wander over him. His hair, though damp, was combed back, and he'd neatly trimmed his mustache and beard, which emphasized his handsome face that had a beautiful, genuine smile. He wore a long-sleeved black shirt and khaki pants, which he wore well. She knew that she had fallen for him before she saw him in person, and now that he stood in front of her, those feelings of attraction and affection that she had for him were incredibly strong.

"Are you ready for dinner?"

Maeve stood. "Yep. I already fed Charlie, and he's been out."

Her coat was over one of the chairs. He picked it up and held it for her to slip her arms in. And when they reached his truck, he opened the door for her. He had manners that many men no longer had. She was impressed by his simple courteous actions.

Dinner

Alex insisted on driving to the restaurant. Maeve sat in the passenger seat, gazing at him as he drove. It felt exhilarating to be going on a date with him. It was his first night home, and dinner with her was how he wanted to spend it. Although it should have felt awkward, it didn't to either of them.

The hostess sat them at a booth in a quiet corner of the restaurant.

"Do you drink red wine?" he asked, realizing he didn't know many of her preferences.

"Yes, and it goes well with a steak," she said, gazing at him over her menu from across the booth.

"I'll get a bottle. Is a cab blend okay?"

"Sounds good," she said. "This is much better than the soup I had planned. Thank you again for the dinner invitation."

The server brought their bottle of wine. After he tasted it and approved the bottle, the server poured them both a glass. Alex lifted his glass to her. "To our first date."

She chuckled with him and tapped his glass. "Our first date." Then she tasted it. It was smooth and would go well with the filet mignon she'd ordered.

The conversation flowed as easily as it had through text message and email. At Alex's prompting, they made plans for living together, for sharing costs and housework. She found it refreshing that he insisted on paying for half her monthly expenses and he committed to taking on his share of the house and yard work, which she'd have whether he was there or not. He again promised to be the perfect houseguest, and he assured her that she'd never regret inviting him to stay.

"I'm sure all will go smoothly, Alex. It's only for six weeks."

"You don't know how much you are helping me, again," Alex insisted. "And to be honest, I love the idea of getting to spend so much time with you. You're not the only one who got used to us talking every day, well through email and text. But you know what I mean." He reached across the table and took hold of her hand. "Maeve, if I were able to move home, I'd probably still text or call you every night before bed. I'd miss the communication. I'd miss you."

Maeve's heart did a little flip in her chest. "I'd miss you too," she admitted. "It's weird. It's like I know you so well, but to have you physically here with me is crazy." Crazy exhilarating, she thought. She couldn't stop smiling.

"I know," Alex agreed. "It's got this feeling of a new relationship, yet it feels comfortable like we've always been friends at the same time. All I know is that for a long time, I've wanted to hold you and kiss you and sit with you like this out for dinner while holding your hand," he said, giving her hand a squeeze. "And it feels surreal to be doing it now."

"Yes, that's exactly what it feels like, surreal."

The server brought their appetizer, stuffed mushrooms. Alex served her a couple before taking two for himself. He dug in, famished and excited for good food.

Maeve watched him with delight as he cut the large mushroom caps in half and shoveled them into his mouth. He made sounds of approval as he ate.

"Oh my God, this is so good," he said.

Maeve chuckled. "Was the food over there that bad?"

"No, it just wasn't this good. It was okay, some things better than others, with very little choice, and many meals repeated. The turkey dinner they cooked up for Thanksgiving wasn't terrible, but let me just say I'm happy I won't have to have Christmas dinner over there."

"What are your plans for Christmas?" she asked. "You said your parents and sister are in Florida. Are you going to see them over the holidays?"

"No, I didn't make plans to go, not knowing if I'd be back or not. And last-minute airfare is so expensive, not to mention that I'll just be getting back to work. It would be wrong to ask off, though I technically could delay going back to work for a few weeks, but that doesn't feel right either. What about you? You said your parents are in Arizona and your brother is a doctor in Chicago, right?"

"My parents invited me, but I didn't want to leave Charlie in a kennel or at Animal House over the holidays. My brother's not going this year either. Even though he probably has the seniority to take off, he's a workaholic and wants to be the head of his department, which means working every holiday."

"Do you have plans with friends?" he asked.

"Michelle invited me and Charlie for dinner. I know you'd be welcome to join if you'd like," she said with a smile.

"As I have no plans, crashing your Christmas dinner sounds good, if you don't mind, and provided your friend, Michelle, is okay with it. I'd like to meet her and her husband," Alex said.

She laughed. "It has to feel weird, just getting back so close to Christmas."

"Yes, it does, especially since up until a few days before we packed up, I didn't know I would be back. But there is always this weird adjustment period when I get back from deployment. I guess it'll just be a little weirder this time around because I can't go back to my own house. I really appreciate your offer to stay with you, Maeve."

"It'll be good for Charlie and I'm glad I can help you."

"You are." He smiled warmly at her. She was his hero. First for taking Charlie and now for letting him stay too. He'd have to figure out a really great Christmas present for her. "Are you off work at all over the holidays?" he asked.

"A few days, Christmas Eve and Christmas Day and of course New Year's Day. I have to work a half day on New Year's Eve."

"On New Year's Eve, we should find a party. The Sports Spot usually has one," Alex said. "I'm sure Steve will be there."

"That would be fun," she agreed. "I'll check into it tomorrow."

Their dinners arrived. The porterhouse on Alex's plate was massive. There was also a large baked potato. Maeve's filet looked and smelled delicious. She'd also gotten a baked potato, which took up half her plate. She'd never been to this steakhouse before. It was on the outskirts of Norfolk.

"Everything looks good," she said. "This is one of the fun parts of meeting someone new, discovering new restaurants."

"I look forward to discovering your favorite places too," he said.

They continued to enjoy the easy conversation throughout dinner as they ate. With takeaway boxes in hand containing their leftovers, they stepped out into the cool night and into the flurries that fell from the sky. It was beautiful. There was no breeze, and the entire area was quiet.

Alex followed Maeve to the passenger side of the car and opened her door. Before she slid into her seat, he leaned in and kissed her. "Thank you for being my dinner companion this evening."

"Thank you for the invitation and for paying." She'd offered to split the check, but he refused. He wouldn't allow her to leave a tip either.

"I invited you; it's only right."

"Please don't think you owe me, because you don't."

He gazed into her sparkling brown eyes. "I invited you because I wanted to spend my first dinner home with you and only you. And I paid because I was raised to be a gentleman. My mom would scold me if I didn't pay on a date. Or if I didn't open the car door for my date." He nodded to the inside of the truck, and he closed the door after she was inside.

Maeve watched him cross in front of the truck and take his place behind the wheel. She was impressed with his manners. His mother had raised him well. The other thing she'd noticed was that he never looked at his phone throughout dinner. That was one thing that really bothered her about most men she'd dated. They usually laid their phones on the table beside them and answered text messages and even took phone calls while out to dinner. Michael did it on a regular basis, and she told herself it meant nothing and it was just a bad habit.

He parked in her driveway when they arrived at her house and walked her to the front door. "So, at this point in the evening, I would be giving you a goodnight kiss, and I'd be wondering if I'd be invited inside." He smiled at her and maneuvered her so that her back was against the side of the house. He caressed her cheek with the back of his hand. "Call me traditional, but I'd still like to have that kiss on your front porch to officially end our date."

She returned his smile; her gaze locked on his. "Before we go inside," she said.

He leaned in and kissed her slowly, softly. She'd later compare it to the fantasized kisses she'd conjured and be blown away at how incredible the real ones were.

He stepped out of her personal space after he broke from the kiss. He easily could get lost in her. He wanted to take it further than she had indicated she was comfortable with, but he would wait however long it would take for her to want it too.

She fumbled with her keys, unlocking the door. "I'll have to find my spare set of keys for you to have," she said.

They stepped inside, and Charlie rolled from the couch and came over to greet them.

Maeve crossed through the kitchen. "Come on, Charlie, let's go out."

Alex stepped out of the back sliding glass door with her and into her backyard. It was just as it looked in the pictures and videos that she'd sent of Charlie playing except now there were Christmas decorations back here too. There were lights strung on the trees and in garland at the top of the fence. It looked beautiful with the snow flurries falling.

Charlie trotted back after doing his business, and the three of them went back inside. "I wonder if the snow will accumulate at all. It looks like it's melting as it hits the ground."

"It's kind of early for measurable snow, isn't it?" Alex asked.

"Yes, probably. Just wishful thinking on my part," she said.

They stood awkwardly in the kitchen for a silent moment.

"If you don't mind, I'm going to head to bed. I'm beat. I hope I can get on the right time schedule within a day or two."

"I hope you sleep well," she said. "I'll probably watch TV in bed for a bit before going to sleep. I'll see you in the morning, Alex. Please make yourself at home if you're up before me." She showed him where the coffee, mugs, and silverware were. "Feel free to open any cabinet or drawer."

"Thanks, I will."

She turned the lights off and locked the house up. The two of them walked into the short hallway. And once they arrived in their rooms, almost at the same time, they both called for Charlie. Charlie's gaze shifted between them, back and forth and then back and forth again. He sat where he was.

"Oh, yeah. You'll want him to sleep with you," Maeve said, disappointed.

"You can take him with you tonight," Alex said. "I had him during my nap. Charlie, go with Maeve," he said, pointing to her.

Charlie didn't move.

"Charlie, come on," she called and clapped her hands.

Charlie still didn't move.

Alex walked past him, towards Maeve's room. "Come, Charlie."

Charlie followed him. Inside, he jumped up onto his spot on Maeve's bed.

"We could switch off every other night, if you like," she said. Though she knew at some point, she had to get used to Charlie sleeping with Alex. When Alex left at the end of January, he'd take Charlie with him.

"Sounds good," Alex said. He gave Maeve a kiss on the cheek. "Sleep well." He closed the door on his way out.

Maeve didn't lock the bedroom door. She felt perfectly safe with Alex in the house. She slept well, snuggled with Charlie.

When she woke the next morning, it was to the smell of freshly brewed coffee. She was momentarily confused in her just-waking haze before she remembered that Alex was staying with her. She got up and put on a pair of yoga pants and put on a sports bra, tank top, and a hoodie as a run was on her morning agenda. Getting dressed first thing was not her normal routine, but it felt necessary with him in the house.

She and Charlie entered the kitchen. Alex sat at the table. "Good morning," she greeted him.

"Good morning."

The blinds on the sliding glass door were open. There was no snow on the ground. Alex stood and opened the door. "Come on, Charlie, let's go out."

She poured a cup of coffee and stood by the counter, watching him through the glass door. His hair was disheveled from sleep, and somehow, he looked even more handsome. He wore a beige sweatshirt and black sweatpants.

"How did you sleep?" she asked when he stepped back into the house with Charlie.

"Good, thank you. I woke up pretty early. I hope I didn't wake you."

"No." She took a sip from her mug. "Thank you for making coffee."

"You're welcome. It's good. That was something else that was not so great over there," he said with a small chuckle.

"What are your plans today?" she asked.

"I need to drive into Norfolk to the base and complete some administrative paperwork. Then I'll go by my house and pick up some things, clothes, a few personal items, my work gear. I'll probably pop into work and arrange the day I'll be back full-time. What about you? What does your day look like?"

"Monday morning, back to work. At some point this morning, I want to take Charlie for a run. Would you like to join me?"

A grin spread wide on his face. "I'd love to. First, how about I make us breakfast? I have already checked your fridge. You have the ingredients. Would you like a vegetable omelet?" He was starving, but he had waited for her to eat breakfast. He wanted to cook for her.

"I'd love one, thank you."

She fed Charlie his breakfast as Alex got busy chopping vegetables. Then she sat at the table and enjoyed her coffee as he whipped up the veggie omelets. "I could get used to this," she joked.

He laughed. "I'll be out the door for work most mornings before you're up, I'm sure, but on my mornings off I will happily make us breakfast. I love to cook."

"I was joking."

"I know, but I wasn't. I do like to cook and I'm pretty good at it." He beamed her a grin. "Hey, do you like lasagna? I have a taste for it, and I make a good one. I plan to stop at the grocery store while I'm out today and pick up a few things. I can pick up the ingredients and make it for dinner. And let me know of anything else you'd like me to pick up while I'm there."

"Wow, you just might be the best roommate I've ever had."

He shot her a big smile. "That's my plan."

She returned his smile and chuckled. "Lasagna sounds good, thank you. Oh, and pick up some garlic bread to go with it."

"I'll add it to my grocery list," he said as he scrambled two eggs. He made two perfect vegetable omelets and set them on the table.

"Wow, the presentation is beautiful," she said. She'd watched him flip them in the air to turn them, a skill she didn't possess.

"Thank you," he said, taking the seat across from her.

Just as at dinner the previous evening, it was comfortable sitting together while eating and the conversation came easily. They decided to put the run off until after Maeve's workday was complete so she could immediately get to work, and Alex could get going to run his many errands.

It was early afternoon before Alex returned to her house with seven grocery bags, two bins of his clothing, and all his gear for work.

"Looks like you bought the store out," Maeve said, coming up beside him in the kitchen.

"I took an inventory before I headed out this morning and thought I'd get you stocked up on anything I saw you were running low on."

"That was very nice of you, Alex."

"Well, remember, I'm going for best roommate ever," he said with a laugh.

She chuckled with him. "How'd things go when you stopped in at your job?"

"Good. I'm going back full-time on Wednesday."

"Wednesday of this week? As in the day after tomorrow?"

"Yes, they could use the help this week, got a few guys out sick." He shrugged. "It was inevitable, had to go back sometime."

They put the groceries away. Not only had he stocked her up on all her staples, including laundry detergent and all paper products, he'd bought a lot of food items she normally didn't. Her cabinets and the refrigerator and freezer were all stuffed full when they'd got everything put away.

Maeve took hold of both his hands. "Alex, thank you for doing this. I appreciate it." She reached her lips to his and gifted him with a kiss.

Daily Life

They settled into a comfortable and natural routine between when he'd gotten back and Christmas. Alex went along with her to her bowling league and met her friends. He fit in well with them; she noted. He volunteered to be a sub if needed but was happy to sit near the team and socialize. On nights they were home together, they watched television snuggled on the couch, holding hands or just sitting beside each other. He did try to always maintain physical contact with her, which was never a problem for her.

A good morning kiss on days they were both up together before he left for work became a part of the routine, just as a good-night kiss before they separated to their respective bedrooms had become the norm. Several times their kisses had escalated past the PG range, which she put a stop to. Alex was perplexed as to why the natural progression of a physical relationship wasn't occurring. Emotionally, they were getting closer every day. But he respected her reticence and was hopeful that soon she'd trust him enough to allow more intimate contact.

He went with her one day when she volunteered at Animal House Shelter. Despite the horrible memories of having to leave Charlie that day, he was also flooded with the joy of adopting Charlie there as they pulled into the parking lot. When they passed through the doors, he was greeted warmly by Elyse.

"Alex, Maeve told me you'd gotten back," she said as she embraced him.

"Hello, Elyse, yes. It was a long six months."

"I'm sure Charlie was happy to see you," she said.

"Not as happy as I was to see him and meet Maeve in person. I owe you so much for taking care of him and placing him with Maeve."

"She volunteered to foster him right after you walked out the door that day," Elyse said. "That was the fastest we ever placed a dog in foster care."

"He and I both lucked out," Alex said. "Well, I am here to volunteer with Maeve today. It's going to be hard for me not to take a few more home with me." He chuckled.

"You haven't won the lottery yet," Maeve said. "So adopting three or four more is off the table," she said to him. "Besides, Charlie is a happy only child."

Alex gazed at Elyse and nodded. "That he is."

"Where do you need us today, Elyse?" Maeve asked.

She pointed at the door that led to the kennels. "Kennels need cleaning and dogs need playing with. I'm happy to have you both here today."

"Glad to help," Alex said.

They put in several hours' work cleaning the kennels and then play-ing with a group of dogs in the outside pen. Alex found it rewarding. He understood Maeve's motives for the volunteer work she did there. He promised to come help again when his schedule again allowed it.

They stopped at the coffee shop on their way home. "I stopped here with Charlie that day," Alex said. "I got him a pup cup, and we sat on the patio. I barely held it together, knowing I was bringing him to the shelter," he confessed.

"I stopped that day too, like I do most days either before or after my shift, but I distinctly remember going through the drive-thru before going to Animal House the day I brought Charlie home. Alex, we were probably here around the same time that day."

He chuckled and took a drink of his coffee. "I wasn't looking at anything or anyone except for Charlie that day. You could have sat at my table across from me in your sexy pirate costume and I wouldn't have noticed."

She reached across the table and took his hand. "Are you okay? Was that too much for you, going back to Animal House today?"

"The short answer is, I'm glad I did. You know, Maeve, while serving, I've seen animals and people blown up, people shot, people killed. As a tree trimmer, I saw a guy fall out of a tree and become impaled on a fence. I've seen chainsaw accidents that I won't describe to you because they were so horrific, but I think the worst PTSD I suffered came from having to leave Charlie at that shelter."

Seeing how sad he looked; she got out of her chair and took the one beside him, and she wrapped her arms around him. "Alex, I'm so sorry."

"But when you wrote me and told me you had him and you sent me all the pictures of him, I knew he was being loved and cared for as well as I cared for him. That helped. When the feelings hit me, all I had to do was look at one of the pictures you sent. And when I did, my stress and anxiety, and if I'm being honest," he said and then paused, collecting his thoughts. "When the crippling sadness I felt when I left him in that kennel and walked out that door hit me, it was far worse than stress or anxiety, but the pictures of Charlie living his best life with you helped."

Maeve's heart ached for him. "But you're back now, and you know if you ever have to leave him again, he's always got a place with me."

"I filed my separation papers," he said.

Her breath hitched in her chest. "You did?"

"I don't ever want to leave Charlie again."

His sad eyes stared deeply into hers, and she thought she saw something else there, something he wasn't saying. "I thought you hadn't come to a decision yet."

"My buddy, Darren, and I were on patrol clearing some buildings, and our explosives-sniffing dog, Victor, didn't alert fast enough, or Darren didn't read it; I'm not sure which. Maybe the trigger was farther from the device than we thought; I don't know."

Maeve's heart skipped a beat, anticipating what was coming next. Tears pricked at her eyes, burning them.

"Darren lost an arm, and Victor bled out. It just as easily could have been me. I never worried about that before, but I never had someone in my life that I wanted a future with like I want one with you, Maeve."

Warmth spread through her, a giddy feeling that didn't match what he'd just shared. She pressed a kiss on his cheek and then dropped her head against his shoulder. "I love you, Alex. I would never ask you to choose between serving and me. I'm not going anywhere."

"And neither am I, and not back on deployment, that's for sure."

When they returned to her house, he kissed her once they were in the living room with the door shut. He needed physical closeness. His emotions still felt raw from being at Animal House and from the discussion they'd had. He wanted to make love to her. He needed to make love to her. But she stopped it again.

Not understanding why she couldn't take that step with him, despite his patience, several days before Christmas, Alex reached out to their mutual friend Steve and arranged to meet him for a beer after work. He entered The Sports Spot and found Steve at the end of the bar.

"Hey, long time, no see," Steve greeted. He came to his feet and embraced Alex in a hug.

"Nice to see you," Alex said. "Maeve tells me you and Jill are back together. Congrats, dude."

"Thanks, yeah, we both finally pulled our heads out of our asses." Steve laughed.

"That's great and about damn time." Alex sat and ordered a beer.

"When did you get back?"

"A few weeks ago. The guy I rented my house to can't be out until the end of January. I'm staying with Maeve."

"No way! I hadn't heard." Steve eyed him with curiosity. "And how's that going?"

Alex chuckled. "Good. She's great. Why didn't you ever introduce her to me?"

"Are the two of you?" he asked, stopping short from completing the question.

"Kind of," Alex said. "We're sleeping in separate bedrooms, if that's what you're asking. Not my idea."

Steve laughed as the bartender set the beer in front of Alex. "But you're kind of together?"

Alex took a drink. "Yeah, it's an odd relationship. We've gone out on several dates, we eat dinner together every night, watch television all cuddled up on the couch, and I've gone to bowling with her. We've even gone to the grocery store together. We get along great and it feels perfectly compatible. We're living together without the sleeping together part. She said she needs to take it slow, which I respect, but I really like her, dude, and it's getting hard to keep it in the PG zone."

"Did she tell you about her douche ex-boyfriend?"

"Nope," Alex said. "I figured it was either something like that or she'd been attacked."

"I'm not aware of any attacks or anything, but he did a number on her. She walked in to find him in her bed with another woman less than a month before their wedding."

"Wow, that's lousy. Wedding? So he wasn't just an ex-boyfriend, he was her fiancé?"

"Yep, a total douche. Maeve is great, and it sucked seeing her hurt. But she didn't accept his apologies, and she ended it. I respected her for that. What really sucked though, was seeing her self-confidence take a hit from it."

Alex took another drink and rolled it around his brain. Everything suddenly made sense. He nodded.

"She asked me about you a few months ago."

"She did?" Alex asked, surprised.

"Yeah, I was hopeful that she was getting over what the douche had done to her when she asked. It was obvious she was interested in you, asked me what kind of guy you were."

"And what did you tell her?"

"I don't remember," Steve said with a smile as he lifted his beer bottle to his lips.

"You suck," Alex told him.

Steve laughed. "She's been taking care of your dog and has been in a long-distance relationship with you ever since, so it couldn't have been too bad."

"So, she hasn't been seeing anyone?" Alex asked.

"As far as I know, she's been a nun for the last year since she broke off the engagement."

"You don't think she has any unresolved feelings left for him, do you?"

Steve laughed. "No. Anything she felt for him evaporated a long time ago. I don't think she even harbors murderous feelings towards him any longer."

"That's good," Alex said with a laugh. "But I can't see her with murderous intentions."

"No, she's a gem. So, what are you going to do about her?"

"Prove to her I'm trustworthy."

"One more thing," Steve said. "Sorry, but she kind of knows about Ashley. Ashley was here for the band we came to see Labor Day weekend and Jill kind of exploded that she had nerve showing her face here. She let it slip who Ashley was. I could see Maeve watching Ashley most of the night, no doubt comparing herself to Miss Virginia."

"Jill didn't tell Maeve that she was a Miss Virginia, did she?"

"No, and we were sure to tell Maeve that she may be pretty on the outside but she's fucking ugly on the inside."

"No shit, that's an understatement. I wish she didn't hear about Ashley that way. No woman wants to be a guy's next relationship after he breaks up with an actual beauty pageant winner. I haven't told Maeve about her. We haven't talked about our exes at all. I guess we're going to have to."

"Sorry, man," Steve apologized again.

"It's okay."

"Did you get her a Christmas present?"

Alex's smile answered the question before he spoke. "Two in fact. One from me and one from Charlie."

"You got it bad for her," Steve remarked.

"She's incredible."

"She is. Good luck," Steve said, raising his beer bottle.

Both men drank.

"By the way, you and Maeve are coming to the New Years Eve party here, aren't you?"

"Yeah, Maeve got the tickets weeks ago."

"The official party starts at eight. Come at seven to my special pre-party. Jill and I want you and Maeve to be there. I think Jill messaged Maeve about it last week."

"We will," Alex said. He finished his beer and then checked his watch. "I better go. It's my night to cook."

"Such a cute domestic couple," Steve teased.

Alex left cash on the bar top beside his empty bottle and left. He rolled around all Steve had said on his way to Maeve's house. Oddly, the question of whether she'd replaced her mattress stuck in his brain. He shook that thought away as he pulled into the driveway.

Maeve was still in her office working when he came into the house. After he poked his head in and said hi, he went right to the kitchen to prepare dinner. Tonight, he was making jambalaya. Everything was chopped and was sizzling in the pan, the aromas filling the kitchen with images of Louisiana, when Maeve finally ended her workday and came into the kitchen.

"Mm, that smells amazing," she said, coming up behind him. She wrapped her arms around his waist and dropped her head against his back.

"Long day for you," he said, turning in her arms so that they now embraced each other chest to chest.

"Yes, one of my clients made a last-minute decision to give Christmas bonuses to his employees. He's going to hand the checks out tomorrow, which is the last day of work before he shuts down until the New Year. So, I had to get all the tax withholding done today and run his payroll. How was your day?"

"It was good," Alex said. He pressed a kiss to the top of her head and inhaled the fresh scent of her shampoo and conditioner. "It's better now." His lips moved to hers. He kissed her softly and slowly.

This time, he was the first to pull away. Usually, it was Maeve. He turned back to the stove and stirred the contents of the frying pan. Then he stirred the rice. Maeve got the plates from the cabinet and set them on the counter beside the stove. She set the silverware and napkins on the table.

"Did you feed Charlie his dinner?" she asked.

"Yes, he's been fed and out."

When the meal was ready, he plated it and they ate. They cleaned the kitchen up together after, as had become another of their routines. Then they settled on the couch and started a movie. An hour later, Maeve had to use the bathroom. They paused the movie while she went.

When she returned to the living room, Alex lay on his side on the couch. He patted the cushion in front of him, inviting her to lie in front of him. She settled in, with her back against his chest, only then noticing that he'd turned the electric fireplace on while she'd been out of the room. She turned her head to look at his face when after a moment, he hadn't restarted the movie.

"These last few weeks that we've been together have been amazing, Maeve," he said. "I want to talk to you about something."

She rolled onto her back and gazed into his beautiful blue eyes, trying to get a foreshadowing of what this conversation could be about. "Sure, what?" She felt on guard, unsure if it was something positive or negative.

"I knew I had fallen for you before I got back from Africa. And spending so much time with you since I've been back has only deepened my feelings for you. Living together has been easy, little adjustment required. For me anyway, I hope you feel the same." He paused, watching the expression on her face.

It was still guarded. She nodded.

He took that to mean that she did feel the same. As he'd promised, he'd really tried to be the perfect roommate. "I've loved getting to know you better."

Maeve braced herself. She was waiting for the but.

"You have to be the most beautiful person I've ever known, both inside and out." He ran his fingers through her hair and pushed a lock from her face.

Her breath hitched in her chest and warmth spread through her from his words. Her body tingled from his touch. She saw only honesty in his return gaze even though she knew for a fact his last girlfriend had been stunningly beautiful.

"I know that I'm in love with you, Maeve," he said, his voice a whisper.

She wasn't sure where her voice went, and her brain froze too. He waited expectantly for some sort of reply. "I, I," she stammered. "I fell in love with you months ago and you being here in person has confirmed those feelings for me."

He leaned in and kissed her, really kissed her. The kiss lasted a long time, and his hands caressed her, daring to go places she'd previously stopped them from going. As things escalated farther than they'd gone, she pulled back, as he expected.

Maeve tried not to be self-conscious about the extra padding on her stomach and on her hips, or when his hand glided over the little roll on her side that bulged over the top of her yoga pants. When his leg slid over her pelvis and his hand ran up her abdomen beneath her shirt, she pulled herself into the couch cushion just far enough to separate their lips.

"I love you Maeve," he repeated, pulling his hand from her shirt. He gripped her hip. "And I want to make love to you. When you're ready." He waited, staring deeply into her eyes. "We've talked about almost everything imaginable through email, text, and in person. Nothing's given me a clue as to why you keep pulling back. I thought maybe you didn't feel the same way I did or maybe you're not attracted to me."

"I do feel the same, Alex and I am very attracted to you. I just don't believe in rushing into that aspect of a relationship."

"Fair enough," he said. He still held her tightly, his face hovering over hers. "Have you ever lived with a past boyfriend?" He could see the discomfort in her return stare with that question.

She nodded.

"I kind of lived with my last girlfriend, well, she had her own place, but she stayed at mine often enough. I want to tell you about her. Her name was Ashley." He saw recognition flare in her eyes. "It ended badly when I found out what kind of person she really was. She had me fooled because she was extremely manipulative and there was always a plausible reason for everything. But when I finally saw her for the shallow, self-centered, narcissist she was, little things that had previously nagged at me about her suddenly made sense. She loved herself far more than she could ever love me. On the outside she was beautiful, and that was where all her energy was focused. She spent a lot of money to maintain that appearance too. She could never go anywhere without hours to do her hair and makeup. I hated that. That's one thing I love about you, that you're not wrapped up in your appearance. You're up for an impromptu trip to the coffee shop, no matter if you've brushed your hair or not. You have depth and substance; you're not just a pretty face. And you are beautiful and comfortable in your own skin which are traits I admire."

"Thank you." She paused. "I actually saw her, Labor Day weekend at The Sports Spot. She was there for the band. Steve and Jill told me who she was. She's stunningly beautiful."

"Not after you get to know her. I look at her now and see nothing but the ugliness inside."

Maeve was bowled over by his honesty. She wanted to tell him about Michael. She knew in her head that it was safe to tell Alex about him. And she would have to in order to fully commit to a complete relationship with him. But her heart had been skewered by Michael's betrayal, a horrible, all-consuming pain that she thought had healed. She also knew that it was her fear of it happening again that kept her from moving forward in a physical relationship with Alex.

"What about your last boyfriend?" Alex prompted.

Maeve closed her eyes tightly, summoning her courage. He deserved the truth from her. She deserved to have a relationship without Michael and what he did to her interfering. She reopened her eyes and stared into his. "We all have our dating horror stories, I'm sure. I almost married mine. I'm glad I found out who he really was before

I did." She paused, trying to put it into words that told him enough but didn't drag on longer than she wanted the story to be.

When she didn't continue, he said, "Any man who had his ring on your finger and lost you is a total moron."

"The word is cheater," she said.

"Oh, damn, Maeve, I'm so sorry. What a douchebag, total scum of the earth." He could see the hurt on her face. "You are kind, sweet, intelligent, and as I said beautiful. Something was very wrong with him to not value what he had in you."

She'd never thought about it that way. "Thank you for saying that."

"I mean it. If someone can't be loyal, they shouldn't get into a committed relationship. It's selfish of them and dishonest to pretend to be something they're not. No one deserves to have someone like that in their life."

"It truly sucked but as I said, I'm glad I found out before and not after we got married."

"How close to your wedding date did you find out?"

"Less than a month before," she said.

"Can I ask you how you found out?"

Maeve enunciated that sound that was a cross between a harrumph and a laugh. "His lease was up on his apartment two months before our wedding date, so he moved in with me. I walked in on him with her. Here in my house." Her eyes snapped closed as if trying to block out the image of it.

"Please tell me I will never meet him because if I do, I can't be responsible for the beatdown I'll give him," Alex said.

"I can't say I'd try to stop you, either," she said. "And no, he moved out of the area after I canceled the wedding. I may have told everyone exactly why it was off so his move may have been due to embarrassment."

Alex chuckled. "Good for you. He deserved it. I'm proud of you for canceling the wedding and breaking up with him. But I'm not surprised. You're no one's doormat."

His words brought a smile to her face. "So, now you know why I want to take a physical relationship with you slow."

"I appreciate you telling me." He pressed a kiss to her lips, just one, with no tongue, and then he raised his head back up, several inches from hers. "I'll be here when you're ready, Maeve. I love you and that isn't going to change. I'll faithfully wait for you to trust in us. But I do have to ask you, are you still open to marriage one day? We've never talked about where we see ourselves in the future. And I'll tell you, that's the one deal-breaker for me, a relationship that can't lead to marriage. I want to get married and have kids one day." He hadn't planned to put it all out there when he started this conversation, but he figured it had to be said. He'd declared his love for her, and it was better to know now if that wasn't a future she saw for herself.

Maeve's heart thumped wildly in her chest. She was sure that if a heart monitor was hooked up doctors would be concerned by the speed at which it beat. "I've always seen myself married and with kids. I won't let Michael strip that future from me because of his selfish, heartless actions."

Alex grinned a proud and satisfied smile. "That's my girl."

"Your girl?" She chuckled. She liked him referring to her as his girl.

"Yes. I have no interest in seeing anyone else. I'd like to think we are exclusive so that makes you, my girl."

She laughed again. "Yes, we're exclusive."

"May I make a wild suggestion?"

She saw a spark in his eyes. Combined with the mischievous smile on his face, she braced herself for what she was sure would be something she'd really have to think about. "Suggest away."

His smile grew wider. "Let's start tonight sleeping in the same bed. Doesn't mean anything will happen. But I want to go to sleep like this, holding you. And I want to wake up the same way."

"Oh, Alex," she began.

"You trust me to be a gentleman, don't you?" His smile was still playful.

She nodded. "Yes."

"It's not the sleeping that gets you in trouble." His eyes still sparkled, and he laughed.

"No, it's not," she agreed, joining with a giggle. "Okay, sure. Let's really confuse Charlie. He's not going to like sharing his side of the bed."

Alex laughed more. "If I know Charlie, he'll want to be right between us. He'll keep anything from happening. Golden retriever birth control."

Maeve laughed freely. She felt lighter than she had before they'd talked, the weight of her past hurts lifted.

After letting Charlie out for the last time, she held Alex's hand, leading him to her bedroom. Even though there wasn't going to be any sex happening tonight, she still felt a bit nervous. She went into her bathroom and put on her pajamas, a large nightshirt. As the evenings were cool, she left on her yoga pants and socks.

After he called Charlie onto the foot of the bed, he went to the hall bathroom and got himself ready for bed too, brushed his teeth and changed into a pair of lightweight sleeping pants. He also removed the henley shirt he wore, leaving the dark blue t-shirt on. Then he returned to her room and closed the door as she'd closed it every night since he'd been staying here. He knew she slept on the righthand side. He settled into the left, beneath the covers.

When she came out of the bathroom, she couldn't help but smile at the sight of Alex and Charlie waiting for her in bed. Alex had been correct, Charlie was in the middle of the bed, his head on the crack between both their pillows.

"Golden retriever birth control," she said.

"Told you," he said, rubbing Charlie's belly.

She pulled the covers back on her side and slid over to Charlie, where she too, pet him. Gazing over Charlie's head, she locked eyes with Alex. "Good night."

Alex rose onto his forearms and gave her a goodnight kiss. True to his word, he called Charlie to the foot of the bed and then he rolled closer to her and wrapped his arms around her. "Good night."

"Let me turn the light out," she said after a couple of enjoyable moments. She pulled herself from his embrace and turned her bedside light off. Then she rolled back over and into him, where she settled in and drifted off into a deep sleep.

Christmas Eve

Maeve was off work on Christmas Eve, but Alex worked half a day. She went into Animal House in the morning and worked for a few hours, getting home just before he did. Alex stopped at the meat market on the way home from work and picked up a rack of lamb. He'd already ran several meat options by her that morning for dinner.

He greeted her with a hug and a kiss when he came through the door. "How were things at Animal House?"

"Good. I'm glad I went in." She lifted the paper cup from the Hounds and Grounds Coffee Shop from the table and took a drink.

"I was thinking, would you like to go to church with me tonight? I've always loved the Christmas Eve candlelight service."

"That sounds nice," she said. "Do you have a church in mind?" She'd stopped going after she canceled the wedding.

"The E-V Free Church in Suffolk?" he suggested. It was where he went with his parents, but he hadn't gone in years. He remembered that they did have a nice candlelight service where they sung Christmas songs on Christmas Eve.

Maeve got a horrified look on her face. "I can't go there, Alex."

"Why not?"

Her face contorted into a pained expression. "That's the church I was going to get married at."

"Oh, sorry. Was it his church?"

"No, it was mine. My family went there as long as I can remember."

"Mine too," Alex said.

"No way!"

"Yes, my dad was one of the deacons. When I was a kid, we went to Sunday services, Sunday School, and Vacation Bible School every summer."

"We did too. I loved going to VBS, regular Sunday School not so much."

"We would have been there at the same time. Do you remember going to Christmas Eve services there?" he asked.

"Yes, I remember singing the Christmas songs and lighting candles during the last song which was always," she began.

"*Silent Night*," they said in unison and then both laughed.

"How have our lives been so adjacent to each other for so many years and we never really met?" she asked.

"It is mind-boggling," he said. "I'm sure if we were to dig out our old VBS group pictures and point ourselves out to each other something would register."

"I'm still not up to going to the E-V church. How about we go into Norfolk to Flowing Waters? Elyse was talking about it today. That's where her family goes."

Alex scrunched up his face. "That's the megachurch, isn't it?"

"Yes, and Elyse said she was pleasantly surprised when she went there and she likes it. It's big. It's anonymous. I'd see way too many people I know if we went to Suffolk E-V. Michael and I were attending regularly for the few months before we broke up."

Alex brought Flowing Waters website up on his phone. "There's an eight-p.m. service tonight."

"Perfect."

They enjoyed a good dinner and then dressed in nicer clothes to go to the church service. Maeve was excited with the anonymity of such a large church. She knew there was no way she could step foot back inside the Suffolk E-V Free Church. They held hands as they made the long walk from the parking lot into the building. The campus was huge and the parking lots were filled to capacity with people leaving from the earlier service and people like them arriving for the second one.

They entered the massive lobby, which was open all the way up to the roof of the four-story structure. And they gazed at the enormous Christmas Tree in the center of it. People bustled back and forth. Families posed for group photos in front of the tree and the escalators leading up to the higher balconies of the sanctuary were filled with people being transported up and down.

"Have you ever been in here before?" Alex asked her.

"No, you?"

Alex shook his head. "This is really something." His gaze swept through the cavernous space.

To the left were open double doorways and they could see they led into the auditorium. It looked pack full of people inside.

"Well, should we find seats?"

They stepped towards the nearest set of doors. Just as they entered, taking in the enormous amphitheater with the stage, which was decorated for Christmas against the far wall, a familiar face came out of the crowd.

"Elyse," Maeve greeted her with a smile. "Hello and Merry Christmas."

"Hi, I didn't know you planned to come tonight. Merry Christmas to you both." She gave them both hugs. "I wish I knew, I would have saved you seats with my family. It's getting pretty packed on this level. You may have better luck finding seats if you go up to one of the upper balconies."

"Oh, okay, thanks," Maeve said.

They walked back out and into the lobby with her. Elyse pointed across the way to the restroom signs. "I'm just on my way there." She checked her watch. "The service starts in about ten minutes." Then she pointed to the escalators. "Try the second balcony level. It looked like it had the most seats available."

"Thanks," they both said and then headed to the escalators.

Elyse had been correct; there was still seating on the second balcony level. As they entered the auditorium greeters handed them programs and unlit candles with plastic drip protectors at their base. "They get lit during the last song," one woman said. "Enjoy the service."

They found two empty seats along the railing of the balcony, which gave them an amazing view of the stage. The service was nothing like either of them were used to, but it was a good experience. The music was concert level and the energy in the auditorium was incredible. The Christmas message from the pastor was contemporary. All around them people stood and sang, swayed with the music, and obviously enjoyed the evening.

The final song was the traditional *Silent Night* with the lighting of the candles. The sight of thousands of candles lit, was breathtaking. The voices of so many in the audience joining the chorus on stage, softly at first but rising in volume as the song progressed, was heavenly.

When Maeve and Alex exited into the night air afterwards, they were both energized and felt the Christmas spirit flowing through them. Holding hands as they walked to the car, they agreed Christmas Eve service at Flowing Waters was the best service they'd ever been to.

"I hope it does snow tomorrow, as forecasted," Maeve said. "It would have been nice to have flurries as we left church though."

"A kid at heart. I knew it," Alex joked. He opened the car door for her and closed it after she slid in.

They held hands as he drove to her house. After that beautiful Christmas service, both would agree that they felt emotionally closer than ever. Maeve was grateful they'd had the conversation about their exes as that honest dialog allowed her heart to open, and it deepened her trust in him.

Christmas Morning

They woke up early. It was still dark out. As they were both wide awake, they got up. It was just before six a.m. When they opened the sliding glass door to let Charlie out, they found the forecasted snow had come in early. Outside the yard was already blanketed in a pristine first measurable snowfall of the season that made the world look perfect. Flurries still fell, adding to the magical effect of a Christmas snow globe. They stepped outside into the backyard with Charlie and took in the beautiful sight. The lights she had strung on the fence and over every tree and bush in the yard glistened in the snow. It was quiet and peaceful; the air was calm.

"Wow, this is just beautiful," Maeve said in a whisper as speaking at a regular volume would intrude on the peaceful surroundings.

"Merry Christmas, Maeve," Alex said very softly.

She turned to him, and they shared a Christmas kiss. In that moment all was right with the world.

Charlie ran around the yard, frolicking in the snow. When the three of them stepped back into the house, Maeve started the coffee. After it was brewed and they each had a steaming cup in their hands, they settled on the couch together to exchange gifts.

"This one is from Charlie," Alex said and he handed the package to Maeve. She opened it to find a pair of running shoes, identical to the pair she loved. "You said you need to replace them before the 5K."

"I do, thank you Alex," she paused and laughed. "I mean Charlie." She hugged the dog, who sat on the floor between them. "This is really sweet of you." She leaned over and placed a kiss on his cheek. "And now, you open your gift from Charlie."

Alex chuckled. Charlie had never given him a Christmas gift before. He opened the box to find a 3X6 dashboard mount calendar with pictures of Charlie in fun month appropriate shots, for each month of the year, with captions like she'd sent to him. "Oh my God, this is great."

"I thought you may like to continue to see the pictures of him," Maeve said.

Alex smiled a big, genuine grin. "Thanks, Maeve. It's perfect." Then he handed her another box. "From me."

"You didn't need to. The shoes were a lot."

He nodded at the box, urging her to open it. As she opened the gift, he held his breath.

"Oh my God! Alex?" she asked, her gaze locking onto his.

He was nervous until he saw the smile draw her lips up. "You want to learn to paddleboard, don't you?"

"Yes," she said with a huge grin. "Cancun?" She held the airline tickets up.

"I haven't made reservations at a resort yet. I have two or three in mind, but you get to decide which you want to go to. I know I can be off those dates, but we can change it if you can't get off that week."

She read the dates, middle week of February. She nodded. "I should be able to take off. But this is way too much."

Alex kissed her and held her in his arms after. "It's not too much. It doesn't even come close to being too much. I told you, I'm in love with you, Maeve."

"I love you, too, Alex," she whispered and then initiated another kiss.

It was as though he knew how far to go with the kiss and he pulled back right before she'd reached her intimacy limit, which she appreciated. Though she would admit that she was getting very close to trusting him enough to give in to her intense desire to make love with him.

Her gift to him was left beneath the tree and she felt foolish for its contents after the airline tickets to Cancun from him. She'd had a hard time figuring out a gift for him to begin with.

Alex unwrapped the paper and smiled. Folded inside was her team's bowling shirt. "Does this mean what I think it means? A member of the team?"

"Yes, Joe, the guy with the ponytail, just let us know he got a new job and will be travelling nearly every week. The rest of the team all agree. We want you as our fifth if you want to join us." She smiled, hoping he'd agree.

He embraced her, crushing the package between them. "Yes! This is great. Though I planned to keep coming with you anyway."

"There's dues each week, which I'll pay as part of this gift," she said. She hadn't planned to do that when she'd wrapped the shirt but given his generous gifts of the shoes and the trip, it was the least she could do.

He whipped up a wonderful Christmas breakfast, vegetable omelets, hash brown potatoes and bacon. It was the first delicious meal they'd have that day. Christmas Day dinner at Michelle's house was always a culinary masterpiece.

Maeve's parents called, and she put the phone on speaker. They had a nice conversation. She had told her mother about Alex, but it was the first time they had spoken with him. She had not told her parents that he was staying there, a fact she cued him in on before she'd answered the call.

She put a call in to her brother, Ricky, but it went to voicemail. She left a cheerful Christmas greeting.

"Are you ready to meet my family?" he asked her later that morning. "I'm going to Facetime my sister. She should be at my parents' house by now."

"Do they know you're staying here with me?" Maeve asked.

"Yes, I said you were a friend."

"And are we sticking with that?"

Alex laughed. "What is your preference?"

She grimaced and nodded. "Yeah, can we leave it at that for now?"

"I probably shouldn't have told you my dad was a deacon of the church, huh?" He laughed again.

"Living with a friend, no issue. Living with a girlfriend they just heard about, very different story," she said.

"Okay, I'll let them in on our relationship slowly, after the New Year," he promised.

He initiated the Facetime call and chatted with his sister for a few seconds before she brought her phone to where his parents sat at the dining room table. She propped the phone against something on the table and stood behind them, capturing all three of them in the frame. They thanked each other for the Christmas gifts. Seated beside him but not in the frame, was Maeve, listening to their conversation.

"Oh, hey, here is the woman who fostered Charlie when I deployed and as I told you, has taken me in too." He moved his phone farther out in front of him and Maeve slid closer. "This is my friend, Maeve," he said. "Maeve, meet my mom and dad, Sylvia and Marty, and my sister, Lisa."

"Hi, nice to meet you," she began with a smile. She paused as her gaze lingered on his mom. "Mrs. R! You taught Sunday School, didn't you?"

"Yes, Maeve Torres," Sylvia said. "I remember you from class. I've never known another Maeve. It's an unusual name that I remember, even after all these years."

"Small world," Maeve said. "Alex and I have found it so interesting that we've been adjacent to each other during so many times in our lives."

Everyone chuckled and remarked about the two degrees of separation being fate or God's will.

Then Maeve's gaze landed on Lisa. She recognized her immediately, and a horrified expression spread not only over Maeve's face but also Lisa's. "You? Oh, my God!"

"Oh, shit!" Lisa gasped.

Alex's parents looked as confused as he did. "What, so you two know each other?" Alex asked.

Maeve flew off the couch as though it was on fire and retreated into the kitchen. Tears were in her eyes, and she couldn't catch her breath.

"Maeve, Lisa? What is it?" Alex asked as he rose from the couch and rushed to the kitchen, following Maeve.

"It was her. She was here in my house in my bed with Michael!" Maeve forced out.

Alex's gaze darted back to Lisa, still shocked and not moving a muscle, with a mortified look on her face in the window of his phone. "Lisa?"

Lisa closed her eyes and covered her face with her hand. "I am so sorry. I didn't know he was engaged until you came in and started screaming. I swear," Lisa said. "I hadn't seen him in years."

Alex put it together who Maeve's Michael was. "Mike Bartlet?" he demanded, his gaze locked onto his sisters. "You saw and slept with Mike Bartlet last year when you were in town for Thanksgiving? Are you fucking kidding me?"

"Alex, language," his father scolded him. Then his eyes shifted to his daughter's, who still stood between him and Sylvia. "Is this true Lisa? Did you?"

Alex of course knew it was. "Why on God's green earth would you ever give him the time of day after he hurt you so badly. Jesus Lisa! He cheated on you too. How could you have done that to another woman?"

"I didn't know he was in a relationship! I never would have!"

Maeve pointed at the phone and shook her head. "I can't, Alex."

"I'll call you later," Alex said, looking at his phone. He disconnected the video call and then turned back to Maeve. "I am so sorry." He stepped towards her, to embrace her.

She held her hands up. "No, I can't."

He stepped into her and practically pinned her to the kitchen counter with his body. "Please don't push me away. I've done nothing to you. I want to help. Let me hold you." He wrapped his arms around her and was relieved when she collapsed into him.

"How could your sister have been the one who he was with? Of all the people in this world, how could it have been her?" Maeve cried. "I'll never be able to look at her and not see that moment." In saying the words, she knew that a relationship with Alex was not possible. She cried harder with that realization.

He knew that was what she meant too. "Whose fault was it that you walked in and found them? It was Mike's. It wasn't Lisa's. If it wasn't her, it would have been someone else." He paused and sighed loudly. "He did the same thing to her back in high school when they went out. He was scum then, and he's scum now. I can't believe she would talk to him, let alone sleep with him." He was completely disgusted with his sister and not just because it had hurt Maeve so badly. He rubbed her back gently. "I guess you never said his last name. I never put two and two together. I can't believe you were engaged to Mike Bartlet. You said your fiancé was from out of the area, so I never thought it could possibly be him. Mike Bartlet went to school in Norfolk."

"We'd been talking about Suffolk high schools. And when you asked if you could have known him from high school, I didn't think you would have known him or known of him like you did Steve and my brother." She breathed out a heavy breath and pulled away just enough to look him in the eye. "Alex, what am I supposed to do about this?"

He pressed a soft kiss on her forehead. "It's okay that you never forget that moment, but you can't let it come between us, Maeve. And you'd said you were glad you found out about him before you married him. In a weird way, you have Lisa to thank for that."

"That'll make for some interesting family holidays in the future, won't it?" She emitted an outraged, disbelieving laugh.

Alex couldn't help but join her in a chuckle of the same tone. "You got past this Maeve and knew that it was his fault and that you deserve better. I'm sorry it was Lisa. I'm sorry seeing her brought those feelings back to you today. Please tell me you think you can get past this."

Maeve dropped her forehead to his chest and took in the sensation of his embrace. "I don't blame her. You're right. It was all on Michael but dammit, Alex, how can I see her or talk to her. She's your sister, it's not like I'll never see her again if we stay together."

He didn't like the way she phrased it with an 'if' statement. "Maybe you do need to talk to her. It could help, you know."

"I can't even think about that right now, Alex." Her voice was pleading.

He caressed her back. "Okay, I understand. I need to talk to her though." His text message alert chimed. He glanced at the screen. It was a text from Lisa.

> I'm so sorry, Alex. Please tell her I didn't know he was with anyone. I never would have If I knew.

"That was a text from Lisa," he said. He read it to her.

"I believe her, but that doesn't make this easier."

"If you don't mind, I'm going to step into the other room and call her."

"That's fine. I need to get in the shower before we get the side dishes we're taking to Michelle's made." She pulled away from him and left the kitchen.

Alex was pleased she was still planning on the two of them going to Michelle's house for dinner. He sat in the chair so he could look outside at the beautiful snow scene in the yard, and he initiated a Facetime call to his sister. He propped the phone up against the salt and pepper mills on the table.

"That was a total shitshow," she said as she answered.

He could see she was in the car. "Are you okay, Sis?"

"Well, I'm on my way home. As you can imagine, Mom and Dad got all over me for being with Mike last year. It was a big blow up and I left."

"Lisa, you need to go back and make peace. It's Christmas Day. You all need to spend it together. This will blow over. It's none of their business at this point. You're an adult, living in your own place. Tell them you love them but to let it go. I'm sure it had to have really bothered you last year when it happened."

"Did it ever. It was horrible, Alex. I had no idea he was with someone, least of all engaged. He told me it was his sister's place, and she was out at a friend's bachelorette party and wouldn't be back until very late. He said he lived in Atlanta and was back for the holiday, lying piece of crap!" There was a pause, and she breathed out a heavy breath. "And then this woman comes in and starts screaming and I figured it out really quick who she was and what Mike was to her."

"I'm sorry, Sis. But seriously, and I'm not judging, why would you hook up with Mike Bartlet of all people?" Okay, yes, he was judging.

"It was the Wednesday night before Thanksgiving. I was out with several old friends. I ran into him in a bar, and we talked and it kind of just happened."

"That's why your mood was off last year on Thanksgiving. I knew you'd gone out, and I thought you were just really hungover."

"Yeah, I was a little of that too, but it mostly had been the drama from the night before. It's not every day a woman barges in when you're in bed with someone and is screaming, calling both of you names, and telling everyone to get out of her house. I was sick to my stomach about it. When I realized she was his fiancé and it was her house, I was so sorry. I remember how horrible I felt when I found out Mike had cheated on me back then."

"He hasn't changed any, obviously."

"Right. Really, please tell her I am so sorry."

"Lisa, she's not just a friend. I'm in love with her," he confessed.

"Oh, shit," Lisa said.

"Yeah, and now she's saying if we stay together."

"She can't hold this against you," Lisa said.

"She isn't. But think about it. She isn't sure she can get past having to see you and be reminded of the worst day of her life. She and I don't live in a bubble. Even though you and Mom and Dad live in Florida, for Maeve and me to have a normal relationship there can't be an issue or any drama between you two. What if we get married? What do holiday's look like?"

"I'll apologize to her face. I'll do anything to try to make this right, Alex."

"I appreciate that. I'll let you know when she might be open to that. She's already said not today."

"I get it. So, what are you doing rest of today?"

"We're going to dinner at her friend's house. What about you? Are you going to go back to Mom and Dad's house?"

"I don't know, Alex."

"When we get off this call, I'll call them and talk to them and make sure they'll drop it with you. You turn around and go back and have a nice Christmas."

"Okay, but if they aren't going to let it rest, you call me back and let me know."

"I promise I will," Alex said. "Merry Christmas. I love you, Sis."

"Love you too," she said and then she ended the call.

Alex lifted the phone from the table.

"That was nice of you," Maeve said, startling him. He turned in the chair to face her. She'd been listening to the call and was impressed with how he not only supported his sister with his words, but he also stuck up for her.

"You heard?"

"All of it. Thank you for sticking up for me and my feelings. I didn't mean to eavesdrop." She nodded to his phone. "You better call your parents before she gets back there."

He reached a hand out to her. When she took it, he pulled her in to sit on his lap before he dialed. He put the phone on speaker.

His mother answered. "Hello Alex."

"Hi Mom. I have you on speaker and Maeve is here with me. I just got off the phone with Lisa."

"Oh, honey, Maeve, I'm so sorry it..." she paused, unsure how to finish her sentence. "Lisa swears she didn't know he was engaged. She should never have been with him," Sylvia began.

"Mom, it's Lisa's business and not ours who she spends time with," Alex said. "I just got off the phone with her. She's on her way back to your house but only if you and Dad drop it."

"We're so disappointed in her," Sylvia said.

"It sounds like it got quite heated after I hung up," Alex said.

"It was ugly," she said. "You know your father."

"Is he there? Let me talk to him."

"He's in the garage. I'll bring my phone to him."

They heard the slightly hushed conversation between his parents as she handed the phone off to him. "It's Alex. He talked to Lisa after she left. Marty, hear your son out."

"I should have known your sister would call you to get you on her side," his dad said.

"I called her to see how she was," Alex said. "Dad, there is no her side or your side. We're a family. But who she spends time with and what she does is her business. Not yours, not Mom's, not mine. I talked her into turning around and coming back for Christmas dinner with you. But you have to completely drop it. And stop judging her. I can't believe she'd talk to Mike Bartlet, let alone that she went home with him after how badly she was hurt by him, but again that's not for me to judge and it's not for you to judge either."

"Alex, her behavior is not right with my beliefs."

"What about your belief of forgiveness? Give her that grace, Dad. It's Christmas."

Marty Richmond let out a long breath. "Well, what's done is done, I guess. As long as she apologizes to your friend, I can let it go."

"She has and they'll talk more at a later time," Alex said. His gaze was locked on Maeve's. "What happened to hurt Maeve wasn't Lisa's fault. It was Mike's. Promise me you'll put this aside for the rest of the day when she gets back there."

"I'll do my best."

Maeve saw the annoyed expression on Alex's face. "Dad, if you can't promise, she's not coming back. Do you want to lose her in your life because of Mike Bartlet?"

"When you put it that way, no."

"Okay, you're good then?"

"Yes, son, I'm good."

"Okay, I'll talk to you later. Have a nice dinner."

"Are you eating dinner there at your friend's house where you're staying?"

"No, we're going over to the home of one of her friends. She and her husband are hosting."

"That's nice. I'm glad you won't be alone. Merry Christmas, Alex. And please pass my Christmas blessings on to your friend."

"I will, Dad. Thank you. Merry Christmas to you and Mom." After he ended the call, he put his phone on the table and wrapped her in an embrace. "I promise we can make this okay."

She was impressed by how he'd handled both phone calls. It was clear that he loved his family. He was a protective older brother and a loving and respectful son. He was also a calming voice and unafraid to speak up. All qualities she found attractive.

When she said nothing, his concern increased. Was the future of their relationship still in question in her mind? "Maeve, do you believe me?"

She raised her head from his shoulder and gazed into his eyes. "Yes, I believe you. The shock is wearing off. That's what it was, a complete shock to see her face. I didn't talk to Michael enough after that night to even ask who she was and it honestly didn't matter what her name was. My only communication with him was telling him I never wanted to see or hear from him again. And I told him to come get his stuff out of my house."

"Did he try to change your mind?"

"Oh, yes, he did. Said it was a last meaningless fling, promised he'd never do it again. He wouldn't even call it cheating. He offered to go to couples counseling, anything I needed to be able to forgive him. I told him I could never forgive him."

"I'm proud of you. It had to make you feel strong and empowered, standing up for yourself."

"In retrospect, I guess. At the time it just hurt so bad."

Alex kissed her, wanting to alleviate all the pain from her life, past, present, and future. "I can't even imagine. But you are stronger now for it, I'm sure. And selfishly, I'm glad you didn't marry him, and I got to know you. I love you, Maeve."

"I love you too, Alex."

Christmas Dinner

"A trip to Cancun?" Michelle asked in a hushed voice as Ron and Alex were in the living room. She and Maeve were in the kitchen.

Maeve felt giddy, telling her. "Yes. Can you believe it?"

"I wish we could go too but you know I can't take off during the semester," Michelle said. She grinned, and continued, "Though I'm sure you want to be alone."

"It's not like that," Maeve argued.

Michelle's facial expression silently challenged her.

"Well, yes, it is, but that isn't the only purpose for the trip. We can have as much solitary romance as we want at my house."

"Have you slept with him yet?" Michelle asked, her voice below a whisper.

"Slept in the same bed, yes, but not what you're asking. I'm close to letting my guard down. I trust him," she confessed.

Michelle looked confused for a moment. "You seriously have slept in the same bed with him, and nothing has happened? What's wrong with you and more importantly, what's wrong with him? Is he gay?"

"He's not gay," Maeve argued. "Believe me he's not! He's respectful of my need to take it slow."

"Jeez, girl, how long are you going to make the poor man wait? He's a nice guy. I knew it the first time I met him."

"Yes, he is," Maeve agreed.

"So, what's your problem then?"

Maeve's eyes looked behind Michelle and locked with Alex's. He and Ron had just come into the kitchen.

"Did you tell her about Lisa?" he asked.

"No," Maeve said. "But I was just going to." She let out a cleansing breath. "So, the woman Michael was with last year in my house is Alex's sister, Lisa."

By the expression on Michelle's face, Maeve knew she was wondering if she heard that correctly and was probably still processing it. "Come again?" she finally said.

"Yes, you heard that correctly. Alex's sister, Lisa, was the woman in my bed with Michael the night of my bachelorette party."

Michelle's gaze went to Alex. "Wow, just wow. I don't know what to say."

"Thank you, Lisa, comes to mind now that the shock of that information has worn off," Maeve said.

Alex smiled, his pride in her evident. "If it hadn't been Lisa, it would have been someone else, I'm sure. Once a cheater, always a cheater." He wrapped his arms around Maeve.

"Small world that it is, Michael and his sister dated in high school, and he cheated on her too. According to Lisa, she ran into him in a bar that night after not seeing him for many years and it just happened. Get this, he told her it was his sister's house and that he was in town visiting for Thanksgiving."

"That jerk!" Michelle exclaimed. "Aren't you proud of me? I wanted to call him every name in the book."

"She got in trouble at school for letting a few F-bombs fly in the teacher's lounge," Ron said and then laughed.

"Yeah, my principal didn't take it well, so I'm really trying not to curse. But seriously, wow, Maeve, you're handling this really well."

Maeve shook her head. "I didn't when I saw his sister in a Facetime call this morning."

"It was a shock," Alex said.

"I reacted very poorly."

"Understandable," Alex said.

"Yes, very," Michelle and Ron agreed.

"So, what's this I hear about a Cancun trip?" Michelle asked, her gaze on Alex. "FYI, I can't take off work during the semester. Summer, spring break, or winter break only. The next trip will be a couple's trip that we plan together," she said in a deadpan voice.

When Alex stared at her with a loss for words, both she and Maeve laughed.

"She's just happy that we're together because she and Ron want another couple to travel with," Maeve said, still laughing.

Alex joined them in laughing. "I selfishly do want our first trip to be just the two of us, but sure, let's plan something for spring break, maybe a long skiing or snowboarding weekend?"

"I knew I liked this man," Michelle said.

Letting the Past Go

One day between Christmas and New Year's Eve, Maeve told Alex she was ready to talk to Lisa. He set up a FaceTime call for them after both women were done with work. He took Charlie for a walk as Maeve initiated the call.

When Lisa's face displayed on the screen of her phone, Maeve tamped down the feelings that hit her just from seeing her. Hurt, anger, betrayal. Feelings caused by Michael. Not Lisa, she reminded herself.

"Hi Lisa, I don't think we've been properly introduced. My name is Maeve Torres," she said, willing her voice to remain unemotional.

"Hi Maeve. It's nice to meet you. You're very important to Alex."

Maeve felt her smile come naturally. "He's important to me too." Which was the only reason she was having this conversation with Lisa.

"I want to start by telling you that I am so sorry about Thanksgiving last year. I honestly did not know Mike was engaged or in any relationship. I promise you I never would have been with him had I known."

"I believe you," Maeve said.

"I should have known not to believe him when he said he was single. I guess I hoped he'd changed from the time I knew him. Unfortunately, I'm one of those people who believe we should forgive, as everyone has the ability to change and be a better person."

"Yeah, and I'm sure some people do."

"Not him though," Lisa said.

"No. I was completely blindsided by it. I never suspected he would ever be unfaithful to me," Maeve said.

"Mike and I dated for over a year. And I found out later he'd cheated on me several times with several different girls over the course of that year," Lisa said. "I lost a really good friend over it. She told me she thought he was seeing someone else about six months into our relationship, and I didn't believe her. Our friendship disintegrated because of it. He was a good liar."

"A liar and a narcissist. He wouldn't even call it cheating. He said you were one last fling, and he didn't know you, that he had met you that night in a bar. You know, he and I talked about past relationships, and your name never came up. I'd think a year of his life would have rated a mention," Maeve said.

"I wonder if your name will come up with his next girlfriend," Lisa said. "I doubt it because there'd be a risk that someone would check his story out. He's not going to tell his next ex that he cheated on his fiancé and probably every other girlfriend he's ever had."

Bile rose in Maeve's throat, and her stomach churned. She thought she was ready to have this conversation. She wasn't. "You're probably right. I'm not sure how it's possible to think you know someone without really knowing them."

"At least you don't have to worry about that with Alex. He's one of the good ones," Lisa said.

Maeve knew her return stare was telling. It wasn't that she doubted Alex was a good guy; it was that she doubted her own ability to judge that. She thought she'd gotten past this self-doubt, but here it was again, popping its insecure little head up.

"He is, and you don't have to second-guess that," Lisa assured her. "It sucks when someone deceives you, doesn't it?"

"Yes, it really sucks. I thought I'd dealt with this," she began but paused, looking for the right words. "This not trusting myself to know if a guy is being honest or not. I mean, I know Alex is an honest person, but I thought Michael was too." She breathed out a heavy sigh.

"I know. It's hard not to think all guys are snakes after Mike, but they're not."

Maeve grinned with an amused expression. "An eternal optimist."

"That's me," Lisa said with a laugh. "No, it's more like I won't let that jerk ruin anything else for me. He won't ruin how I view men and screw up any future relationships for me. I refuse to give him that power."

Maeve hadn't thought of it that way. "I like that way of thinking."

"I'm sure when you found out, well, when you walked in to find Mike with me that it had to hurt really bad. And I'm sure seeing my face brought back how you felt that night. I don't want that to be the case every time you see me. Try to think of it this way instead: that was the last moment of your life that he got to ruin."

"Thank you, Lisa. Yeah, I'll try to think of it that way. And no, I don't want to think about it every time I see you. I actually owe you a thank you. As Alex said, if it hadn't been you, it would have been someone else. A cheater's going to cheat. I'm glad I found out before we got married and it would have been a lot harder to end it, I mean lawyers and divorce because I absolutely would have ended it."

Lisa grinned and nodded. "I wondered about it for several months after, wondered if you kicked him to the curb or forgave him. I'm glad you didn't give him a second chance. I'm not sure if you care or not, but it was horrible for me too. It ruined my Thanksgiving at home with my family because I felt so bad for you and, honestly, I was mad at myself for falling for his bullshit that he was single. But once I put it in my rearview and forgave myself, I had to let it go and not think about it."

"I do care that it traumatized you as badly as it did me, and I'm sorry you were the one there that witnessed my freak out."

"It was justified," Lisa said. "I would have used far harsher language and would probably have been physically violent too."

Maeve chuckled. "Believe me, I wanted to be. I was afraid that if I hit him, I wouldn't stop."

Lisa chuckled too. "You know, on a different topic than violence, even then, I had to believe that it had happened to all three of us for a reason, and now I know it happened to you so that you and Alex could find each other."

"That's a nice thought," Maeve said.

"I believe it's true."

Maeve smiled and nodded.

"So, do you think we can move past this and not let it define our relationship?"

"Yes, I think I can," Maeve said. "I'm not going to let Michael ruin a friendship that you and I can have. You're Alex's sister, and you're important to him. I don't want him to feel he's got to walk on eggshells when it comes to you and me."

"I'm glad. Alex is a good brother. He's also one of my best friends. I'm glad we talked."

"Me too," Maeve said. "So, when is the next time you think you'll be in town?"

"I don't know. With Mom and Dad down here in Florida now, I'd think as far as holidays go we'd have them here if there was no specific reason to go back to Virginia. Are you and Alex planning a trip to Florida anytime soon?"

"I don't think so. We're going to Cancun in February and have talked about a skiing trip over spring break. That's as far out as we've planned."

"Sounds like nice plans. So, I take it you're physically active like Alex, like all the high-adrenaline sports stuff?"

Maeve laughed. "Yes, we like many of the same things. I ran the same 5K he did last spring. We're signed up to run one together at the end of January."

"Sounds like you're perfect for each other. I'm glad. I want Alex to be happy."

"I want him to be happy, too," Maeve said. "And he makes me happy." She smiled as she said it. It felt good to say it aloud.

"You definitely deserve it," Lisa said.

The front door opened, and Alex led Charlie in.

"Speak of the devil, he and Charlie are back from their walk." She gazed at him over her shoulder. "I'm still on with Lisa. Did you want to come say hi?"

He came up beside Maeve, cheek to cheek. "Hi Lisa!"

"Hi Alex. How's it going?"

He scrutinized his sister's face. She looked fine. "It's good. You?"

"Yeah, good. Maeve and I had a nice chat."

His head turned to view Maeve. She looked calm and happy. "Glad to hear it."

"Yes, we did," Maeve confirmed. "How was your walk?"

"It's getting cold out and damp," he said. "I'm thinking it's a good night to turn the fireplace on and watch a movie."

"Sounds like a plan right after dinner," Maeve said with a smile. "And it's my night to cook, so I should probably do that. I'm glad we talked, Lisa."

"Me too," she said.

After the call was terminated, he wrapped his arms around Maeve. "Are you really okay? All good?"

"Yes. I forgive her for her unwitting part in it. It was all on Michael, like I told myself last year. She's a good person, and she's genuinely sorry."

Alex kissed her. "Yes, she is both."

Alex was proud of Maeve that she was able to extend forgiveness to Lisa. He was hopeful the two women could have a friendship, maybe one day even proudly call the other sister-in-law. Every day that he spent with Maeve he fell deeper in love with her.

New Years Eve

Maeve and Alex arrived at The Sports Spot at ten minutes to seven. There were already a lot of cars in the parking lot. They were glad they had come early. By eight, there wouldn't be a parking spot available, and it was cold tonight, so parking in the city lot, nearly a block away, would make for a chilly walk.

They found Steve and Jill on the patio portion of the venue that overlooked the sand volleyball courts, which was now enclosed and heated. A group of about fifty people that included their two young children and both sets of their parents were there.

Seeing who was there, Maeve got an inkling of what this pre-New Year's Eve party was about. "I think they're getting remarried right now," she whispered to Alex.

"Do you really think so?" He glanced around and came to the same conclusion.

"Jill and I want to thank all of you for coming to the New Year's Eve party early. As many of you have figured out, we're getting remarried and wanted to celebrate it with all of you!"

Applause sounded through the room accompanying shouts of congratulations.

They all took seats. Steve and Jill stood along one wall with the officiant; a woman Maeve was slightly familiar with. Her name was Sabrina. She was tall and slender with long straight black hair and multiple tattoos, including a beautiful vine that climbed her neck. Not a traditional pastor by any means, but Steve and Jill were not a traditional bride and groom, either.

"On this eve of the New Year," Sabrina began with a heavy southern accent, "Steve and Jill are entering back into the bonds of marriage. Their story proves that with love and forgiveness, two things God stands for, anything is possible. As their friends and family members, you have seen their lives unfold and each of them grow and transform into the people they are today. God has blessed them with this incredible second chance. I challenge them, though, to see the many firsts they will experience."

Alex reached over and took Maeve's hand. She squeezed his hand and smiled at him.

The ceremony continued. Both Steve and Jill wrote their own vows that spoke about love, forgiveness, and doing better for themselves, each other, and their children. They both promised to put the family first. They also promised to keep God at the forefront of their family.

Maeve listened and couldn't help but be inspired by their vows. She remembered how uplifted she had felt leaving Flowing Waters on Christmas Eve. Maybe she should ask Alex if he'd like to go with her on a more regular basis. She and Michael had gone to church because they had to, to be married in her church, as she'd thought she had to have a traditional wedding. But the Suffolk Evangelical Free Church was no longer her church. And she no longer felt the need to be traditional. But she did feel the need to have God be a part of her life and she felt called to go back to church.

As she listened to the wedding ceremony, she thought that if the time came, she'd like Sabrina to be her officiant too. The woman had a way with words, and it was as though Sabrina was talking directly to her. It was a beautiful ceremony, and Maeve nearly cried when Sabrina pronounced them husband and wife.

Champagne was served, and the couple was toasted. It had been a wonderful way to begin a New Year's Eve party. Steve's mom took the children home before the actual New Year's Eve party started, complete with a band.

"I hope Alex's ex doesn't show her face tonight," Jill whispered to Maeve.

"Let her," Maeve said. "I'd love for her to see that Alex is happy."

Jill giggled. "The best revenge."

"You better believe it," Maeve said. And glancing at Alex talking and laughing with Steve and a few other men he knew, there was no disputing that Alex was happy.

His eyes met hers, and he held her gaze as he smiled at her. Every part of his body and soul warmed as he gazed at her, and there was no doubt in his mind that he loved this woman completely. Over the week since Christmas they had become physically closer, stopping just short of making love. He wanted that connection with her like he'd never wanted anything in his life.

The band played its first number, a high-energy dance tune. Alex made a beeline for Maeve and pulled her onto the dance floor, which quickly became crowded. Maeve and Alex had a great time, dancing and socializing with friends. Their first slow dance proved to them both how in sync they were, moving together so perfectly.

"I love you," Maeve said into his ear, his body feeling perfect up against hers. They fit together as though they were made for each other, and they shared the same rhythm as it flowed through them.

Alex pressed a kiss to her cheek beside her ear. "I love you more than you know. Tonight is perfect."

She held on to him, swaying with the music. Her cheek tingled from his kiss. Yes, the night was perfect.

A snack buffet was put out at ten p.m. and they took a break from dancing and got plates. They sat at a table with Steve's brother, Chad, Maeve's boss, and his girlfriend, Kelly. Maeve didn't socialize with Chad much outside of work, unless they both happened to be at an event Steve hosted, like this one.

"So, if Steve and Jill hadn't gotten remarried today, what would you have done for New Year's Eve?" Maeve asked Chad.

"We probably would have stayed in and watched movies," Chad said. "But when your brother asks you to stand up for him, again, you can't say no," he said and then laughed.

167

Maeve and Alex laughed with him. "This doesn't happen often, two people getting a second chance," Maeve said.

"If anyone can make it work, it's Steve and Jill," Chad said. "I'm happy for them." His gaze swept over Alex and Maeve. "I'm happy for you two also. When Steve told me you two were together, I was surprised, didn't know you even knew each other." His gaze focused on Maeve. "I talk to you almost every day at work and didn't know you were fostering his dog or were in communication with him. That made me realize that I really don't know my employees as people. Somewhere along the way, I lost the connection I had to everyone from when I was just a coworker, before I became the supervisor."

Maeve shrugged. "It happens; I guess."

"I want to change that, spend part of the one-on-one time re-establishing personal connections," Chad said. "Maybe we can do informal team lunches out once a month instead of our in-office meetings that are too stuffy. We have a good team, top performers in all categories and I don't want to lose anyone. Manager evals always ask if your manager cares about you as a person. I've slacked on that. Do you think a lunch meeting a month would be welcomed by the team?"

"Yes, I think so," she said. "Are you buying lunch?"

Chad chuckled. "I can expense it."

"Chad, I have to ask you, back in August when you had us do the peer audits, what was that about?" Maeve asked.

"Honestly, and don't tell anyone else on the team, I received a job offer I accepted. I gave my notice and the partners asked if there was anything they could do to keep me. It came down to money and time off. They also asked me who on the team I thought would be my best replacement. I made my recommendation, but they wanted to see audits done by each team member on another as that is a big part of my job function. In the end, they matched the salary and time off offer from the other company, so I stayed, obviously."

Maeve was surprised. She also wondered who his recommended replacement from the team would have been. "Was it a local company?"

"Local enough, a firm in Virginia Beach."

"Which one?" Maeve asked.

Chad smiled. "I'm not going to tell you. I don't want you to look for a job there, knowing they pay more. You're too important to my team."

Maeve chuckled. "Relax, Chad, I'm not looking for a job. I was just curious."

"Let's just say my looking had nothing to do with anything except for salary. They gave me a raise when I took the manager position and then they froze my salary when everyone else got raises."

"For the record, I'm glad you didn't take the other job," Maeve said.

"Really? You would have been promoted to manager if I'd left. You were my choice, and the partners are impressed with you."

"Really?" she asked.

"Yeah, but I am glad I didn't take the other job. It would have been more stress as I would have had to be in the office full-time. Like everyone else, I like working from home most days."

"Yes, you guys have a pretty sweet deal," Alex said.

"Says the man who works in trees," Maeve said.

"In this colder weather and in thunderstorms it's not so great," Alex said. "But there's nothing I'd rather be doing."

"Are you still in the reserves?" Chad asked.

"No, I filed my separation papers shortly after we got back from deployment." His gaze went to Maeve. "What's here is too important to me to leave again. My deployment days are over. And no more weekends or two weeks a year." He took hold of her hand, which she had resting on the table.

"I won't say I'm not happy about it because I am, but I would have been okay with it had you stayed in," Maeve said. But she did appreciate that he'd filed his separation papers, especially after he'd told her about his friend Darren and the injury he'd suffered during the deployment.

Alex raised her hand to his lips, and he kissed her knuckles. "As I said, you're too important to me for me to leave again."

"And I thought you were talking about Charlie," she joked.

The band came back from a break and music sounded through the patio, making a normal conversation next to impossible. They returned to the dance floor and enjoyed the party. The rest of the night passed quickly and before they knew it, the band announced they were just two minutes away from midnight. They'd do a countdown beginning at thirty seconds till.

Alex and Maeve positioned themselves at the rear of the dance floor, up against a window at the side wall. Everyone joined the band in the countdown. "Three, two, one."

January

"Happy New Year!" everyone yelled, the words thundering through the room accompanied by horns, bells, and other noisemakers. Outside they heard firecrackers and, in the sky, small fireworks lit the darkness with bright whites and brilliant colors.

Before the word 'year' had passed his lips, Alex embraced Maeve and kissed her. It was their first New Year together, and he hoped it would be followed by many more.

Maeve was the first to break the kiss but only to move her lips to his ear. "Happy New Year, Alex. I am so glad your unit got home from deployment so we could have this moment together. I love you with all my heart."

Her hot breath blew across his ear and combined with her words; the sensation instantly warmed him everywhere, causing an intense physical reaction. His jeans suddenly became tight. His lips claimed hers again, and he pulled her more firmly against his body so every part of him pressed against her.

Maeve felt his body, felt his hardness, and her body reacted. Yes, she loved this man. She trusted him. And she wanted him. He was her future, and she wanted to embrace that future. She would when they got home. She was finally ready to have a full relationship with him.

They stayed for another half hour celebrating the New Year with champagne with their friends, and when they left the party, she held his hand as they drove home. The celebratory mood of the evening still coursed through them both. And crackling beneath the high feeling was the mutual desire, which created an electric current they both felt.

Once inside the house, Alex let Charlie out and then locked up the house. They walked to the bedroom together, hand in hand, both of them anticipating the night would continue. They were going to the bedroom, but they would not yet be going to sleep. Once inside, Maeve called Charlie onto the foot of the bed on one side. Then she embraced Alex and pressed her lips to his and let actions convey her thoughts and feelings.

The kiss was different from the others they'd shared. It held meaning, promise, tenderness, and passion. Words were not needed. As clothes were pushed away and his caresses grazed over her body parts that she'd previously stopped them from going to, the physical intimacy they shared further solidified their emotional attachment, creating an intense bond they both felt. And she didn't stop his touches, the connection, the carnal appetite that flowed from them both and was eagerly enjoyed. This first coupling had been worth waiting for.

Lying together after, limbs tangled, and hearts full, Maeve would describe how Alex held her, kissed her, caressed her, and made love to her as absolute perfection. She was at peace in a way she'd never felt before.

Alex pressed a kiss to her lips. "That was amazing. I love you, Maeve."

"I love you, Alex. I'm so glad I fostered Charlie."

He chuckled. "I am so glad you did too. You know, it's going to be nearly impossible for me to move out at the end of the month when my renter finally leaves," he said. The thought of moving out saddened him.

"Then don't," Maeve said. "I've given this a lot of thought. I can't imagine you not living here. It would feel like a step backwards in our relationship."

"You want me to stay?" he asked, a big smile on his face.

"Yes, I want you to stay," she confirmed.

Alex kissed her again, reveling in the incredible sensations. He would never have thought that because of one of the worst moments in his life, when he surrendered Charlie to Animal House Shelter, that he would be led to this moment, which was one of the best of his life.

He reached up and turned the bedside light off and then snuggled her, holding her in his arms.

When they woke the next morning, Charlie was between them from the knees down. But they woke as they'd gone to sleep, in each other's arms. He gave her a kiss, which she returned. Hands caressed, and the desire escalated. He tried to roll onto her, which was impossible with Charlie's location.

"Golden retriever birth control," she murmured and then laughed.

He laughed with her. "I'll let him out and then bring you coffee."

"Let him out and then bring yourself back," she invited. "I'd rather have you than coffee."

"You can have both coffee and me," he said. "And then breakfast. I'll bring you breakfast in bed."

She laughed. "You're going to spoil me."

"You better believe it. That's my plan." He kissed her again. "You have no idea how happy you've made me by inviting me to move in permanently."

"Well, you know I'm attached to your dog." She flashed a grin at him.

He chuckled. "And he's attached to you too. I'd say at this point, he's our dog."

"Yes, he is."

"I'm looking forward to our future together, Maeve," he said.

Her heart melted, and a warm sensation flooded her. "Just over a year ago my heart was shattered into a million pieces, and not only was I unsure if it would ever heal, but I didn't think I would ever trust a man with my heart again. But then Charlie came into my life, which brought you into my life, a stranger who became a friend, who became a very important part of my life. I fell in love with you before you came home, and I can't imagine my life without you in it."

Alex didn't get out of bed. Instead, he pushed Charlie to the far side of it, and he made love to her as he had the night before. Afterward, they drifted back off to sleep.

Blinking her eyes open, her gaze locked on Alex's. His sparkling blue eyes were mesmerizing. Charlie was still in bed with them, lying snuggled between them and content. And then Alex leaned over Charlie and kissed her, the slowest, most intense kiss that silently spoke of true love and of carnal fulfillment.

When they finally got up, they discovered the yard was blanketed in a fresh snowfall. They got dressed and went into the yard with Charlie while he did his business and the coffee brewed.

It was a new year with new possibilities. The future was as bright as the sun, which was shining brightly on the sparkling snow. The air was cool, crisp, and clean. A refreshing airing of the traumas from the past. And Alex was home. It wasn't just Charlie's new home. It was his as well.

1 Year Later

Maeve, Alex, and Charlie stepped into the backyard. It was twelve forty-five a.m. on January first. The snow floated down from the heavy cloud layer, adding to the inch that had already fallen that evening. They'd decorated the yard with more lights than Maeve had ever strung over her fence and over every single bush and tree. The greenhouse was lit up beautifully reflecting off the snow and creating a magical view. Charlie frolicked in the snow as they stood with their arms around each other, taking in the moment.

"This last year has been the best of my life. Thank you for being the most important part of it," Alex said.

Maeve kissed him. "Thank you for making it the best year of my life as well."

And it had been quite a year. The everyday moments of life had been the foundation of a solid relationship that had brought them close, their love deepening and growing.

They ran the 5K together, cheering each other on. They were currently training for a half-marathon.

Their trip to Cancun in February had been a blast. It brought them even closer as a couple. Maeve not only learned to paddleboard, but she became a certified scuba diver too, plunging beneath the waves while she held Alex's hand. Their skiing trip over spring break with

Michelle and Ron had been a fun couple's retreat. The bowling season gave way to their playing together on a sand volleyball team, which led right back into bowling season.

The holidays brought with them new in-person memories to add to the reflections of their long-distance relationship from the prior year. They decorated the house and yard together. They baked his favorite cookies together. And they planned for the Thanksgiving and Christmas holidays with both their families in town.

His parents and sister visited over Thanksgiving, but Lisa did not go out the night before. She stayed in, and they all watched a movie together. Maeve hosted the dinner, inviting several friends from Animal House to join them as well.

Her parents and brother came to town for Christmas. The five of them attended the Christmas Eve service at Flowing Waters Church. Maeve and Alex had made it their church and attended at least once a month that year. The Christmas Eve service felt just as magical as it had the year before, even more so because her family was there with them.

And they'd spent New Year's Eve at the party at The Sports Spot for the second year, agreeing it was a tradition they would continue. Steve and Jill celebrated their anniversary and were still doing well in their relationship, role models of how love and forgiveness can overcome any obstacle.

Charlie charged back to them.

Alex pulled the box from his pocket, which had been there all night, waiting for the right moment, and he dropped to one knee. He opened the box. The lights from the thousands of bulbs reflected off the diamond solitaire within. "I love you, Maeve. Marry me, anytime and anywhere of your choosing."

Maeve was completely stunned. Tears filled her eyes, and she merely nodded, overwhelmed and unable to speak. Alex rose and slid it onto the ring finger of her left hand. Charlie came over and nuzzled her hand, expressing his approval.

From some place nearby, another volley of fireworks exploded, with vibrant colors lighting the night sky. They both chuckled. Someone had just added to the special moment they'd always remember.

"A small ceremony soon, as soon as we can pull it off, without much fuss. Just our closest friends and our family members to celebrate it with us," Maeve said.

"And Charlie," Alex said.

"And Charlie," Maeve agreed. "Because without him, this wouldn't have been possible."

The End

Also, part of the **Animal House Shelter Series** is a Family Drama/Contemporary Romance novel titled **That First Year** that introduced the Animal House Shelter and Elyse Laramie. It's a story of love, loss, family, and resiliency, with hope, tears, and laughter. Available as an Audiobook, eBook, and Paperback. You can get it here: https://mybook.to/ThatFirstYear

Look for more follow-on stories that will be a part of the Animal House Shelter Stories Collection. They, for the most part, can be read in any order with the exception of That Second Year, which must be read after That First Year. Watch for That Second Year, coming at a later date.

If you enjoyed the military aspect of this story, check out Margaret

Kay's Amazon Best Selling Shepherd Security Series. It is a Military Romance, Action and Adventure fiction series consisting of 18 published books as of December 2025 with 6 more novels planned. It is different from this story in that it is realistic, with adult language and content that is violent and spicy, followed by healing and strength on the way to the HEA. Start with Book #1, Operation: Protected Angel. You can get it here: https://mybook.to/ShepSec1

Visit Margaret's website https://www.sistersromance.com/ to learn more. Sisters Romance is the imprint of authors Margaret Kay and her sisters, Charlie Roberts and RK Cary. Please visit and check out all three Sisters Romance books.

Please stay in touch. I love to hear from readers! And remember to check out my sister's books. You can be kept abreast of my sister's work and mine on our website:

Visit our website at: https://www.sistersromance.com/

Email me at: MargaretKay@sistersromance.com

Follow me on Facebook at: https://www.facebook.com/MargaretKayAuthor

Subscribe to the Sisters Romance Newsletter to be kept informed of when my next books are due out at:

Subscribe to our Newsletter

About the Author

Margaret Kay is a wife to her best friend of forty years, a mother of two adult children, a grandmother, and a dog-mom who makes her own dog food. Margaret feels fortunate that she has been able to turn her passion of daydreaming about characters and storylines into books that people want to read. Margaret's husband proudly served 8 years in the United States Navy, and Margaret was a veteran of several deployments, before the internet or cell phones.

All of Margaret Kay's novels are available on Amazon, read for free with Kindle Unlimited. Also available in print and some in audiobooks.

Acknowledgements

I truly say thank you to you, the reader, for choosing this book. If you enjoyed it, would you please leave a review, so others might find this book to enjoy, as well? As an Independent Author, without a publishing house to help advertise my work, I rely on reviews from readers such as you and followers on social media to promote me. Thank you! I would greatly appreciate it.

Thank you to my sisters, RK Cary and Charlie Roberts, who are writing their own Romance books. RK has finished up her Destined & Redeemed series and has several other Science Fiction/Fantasy stories in the works. Charlie is working on a contemporary romance series, the Stevens Street Gym Series. Both have been wonderful friends with the honesty and encouragement that only a sister can give. Check out their work on Amazon! Links directly to all our books on Amazon can be found on our website. The link is below.

Thank you to my wonderful and supportive husband for his patience and love while I spend hours upon hours to research and write my stories. Also, for advising me on any parts of this story requiring knowledge of the military or weapons that I did not have.

Thank you to my mother who shared with me her love of books. As a child, the wonderful example my mother set for me as an avid reader led my sisters and me to write our stories. She has encouraged me to publish, and even though she has passed away, I still thank her for her support in every book.

Thank you to my two adult children, Steve and Rachel. You have both given me wonderful support and I hope I have made you proud!

A big thank you to my girlfriends who have encouraged me and made me feel that I could do this at the times I felt insecure in my ability to accomplish this. You know who you are ladies! You hold a special place in my heart.

Thank you to my editor, who gave of her time selflessly to help me with the grammar, not my strongpoint. And thank you to my ARC Team.